TOP SECRET GRAPHICA MYSTERIES

CASEBOOK: UFOS AND ALIEN ENCOUNTERS

Script by Justine and Ron Fontes

Layouts and Designs by Ron Fontes

Skyview Books

an imprint of

WINDMILL BOOKS

New York

Published in 2010 by Windmill Books, LLC
303 Park Avenue South, Suite # 1280
New York, NY 10010-3657

CREDITS:
Script by Justine and Ron Fontes
Layouts and designs by Ron Fontes
Art by Planman, Ltd.

Publisher Cataloging in Publication

Fontes, Justine
    Casebook--UFOs and alien encounters. – School and library ed. / script by
Justine and Ron Fontes ; layouts and designs by Ron Fontes ; art by Planman, Ltd.
    p.   cm. – (Top secret graphica mysteries)
Summary: Einstein and his friends are joined by Dave from Roswell, New Mexico, as
they use their virtual visors to investigate reported UFO sightings and alien encounters
and possible explanations for the phenomena.
ISBN 978-1-60754-603-0. – ISBN 978-1-60754-604-7 (pbk.)
ISBN 978-1-60754-605-4 (6-pack)
    1.   Unidentified flying objects—Sightings and encounters—Juvenile fiction
2. Human-alien encounters—Juvenile fiction   3. Graphic novels   [1. Unidentified
flying objects—Fiction   2. Human-alien encounters—Fiction   3. Graphic novels]
I. Fontes, Ron   II. Title   III. Title: UFOs and alien encounters   IV. Series
        741.5/973—dc22

Manufactured in the United States of America

CPSIA Compliance Information: Batch #BW10W: For futher information contact Windmill Books, New York, New York at 1-866-478-0556.

CONTENTS

Welcome to the Windmill Bakery

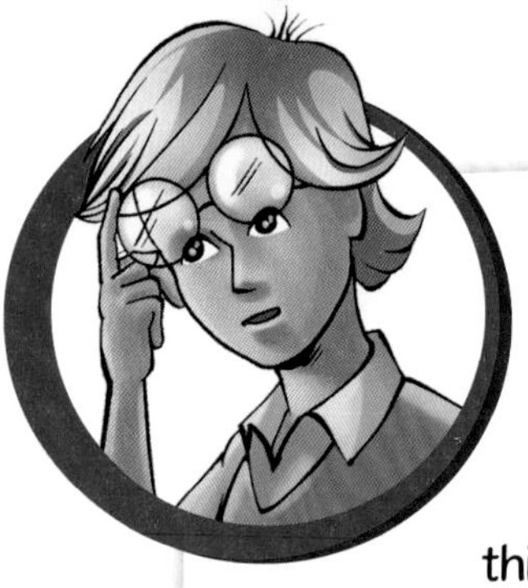

Edward Icarus Stein is known as "Einstein" because of his initials "E.I." and his last name, and because he loves science the way fanatical fans love sports. Einstein dedicates his waking hours to observing as much as he can of all the strange things just beyond human knowledge, because "that's the discovery zone," as he calls it. Einstein aspires to nothing less than living up to his nickname and coming up with a truly groundbreaking scientific discovery. So far this brilliant seventh grader's best invention is the Virtual Visors he and his friends use to explore strange phenomena. Einstein's parents own the local bakery where the friends meet.

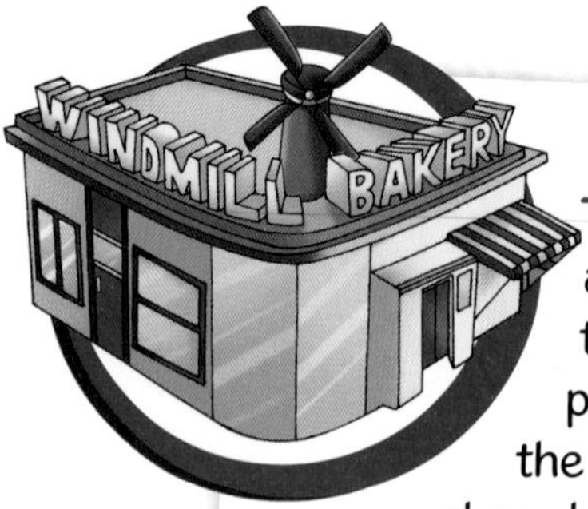
WINDMILL
BAKERY

The Windmill Bakery is a cozy place where friends and neighbors buy homemade goodies to go or to eat on the premises. Einstein's kindhearted parents make everyone feel welcome, especially the friends who understand their exceptional son and share his appetite for discovery!

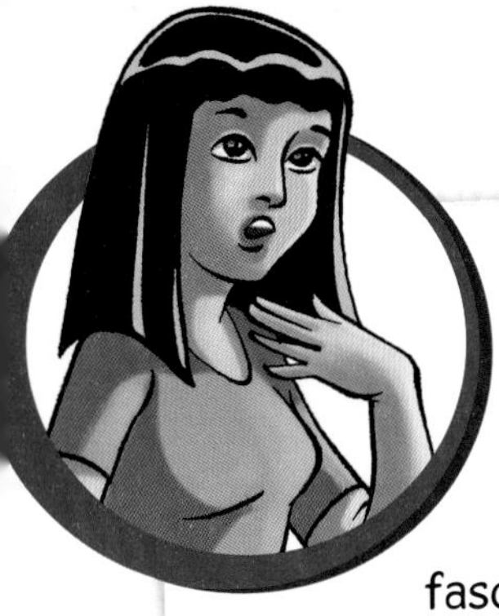

"Spacey Tracy" Lee saw a UFO when she was seven. Her parents tried to dismiss the incident as a "waking dream." But Tracy knew what she saw and it inspired her to investigate the UFO phenomenon. The more she learned, the more fascinated she became. She earned her nickname by constantly talking about UFOs. Tracy hopes to become a reporter when she grows up so she can continue to explore the unknown. A straight-A student, Tracy enjoys swimming, gymnastics, and playing the cello. Now that she's "more mature" and hoping to lose the silly nickname, Tracy shares the experience that changed her life forever only with her Virtual Visor buddies.

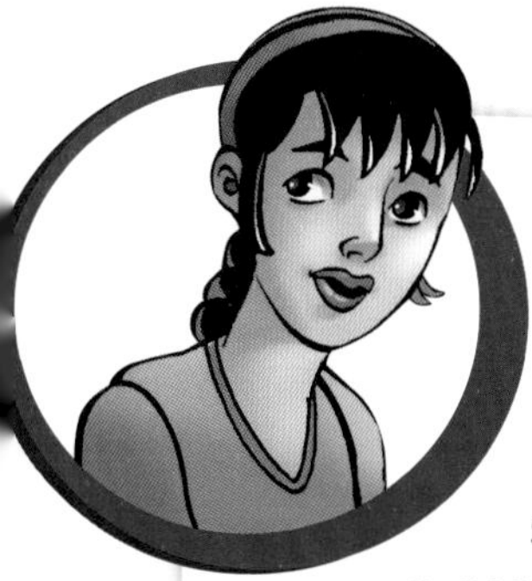

Clarita Gonzales knows that Indiana Jones and Lara Croft aren't real people, but that doesn't stop this seventh grader from wanting to be an adventurous archaeologist. Clarita's parents will support any path she chooses, as long as she gets a good education. Unfortunately, school isn't her strong point. During most classes, Clarita's mind wanders to, as she puts it, "more exciting places—like Atlantis!" A tomboy thanks to her three older brothers and one younger brother, Clarita is a great soccer player and is also into martial arts. Her interest in archaeology extends to architecture, artifacts, cooking, and all forms of culture. (Clarita would have a crush on Einstein if he wasn't "such a bookworm")!

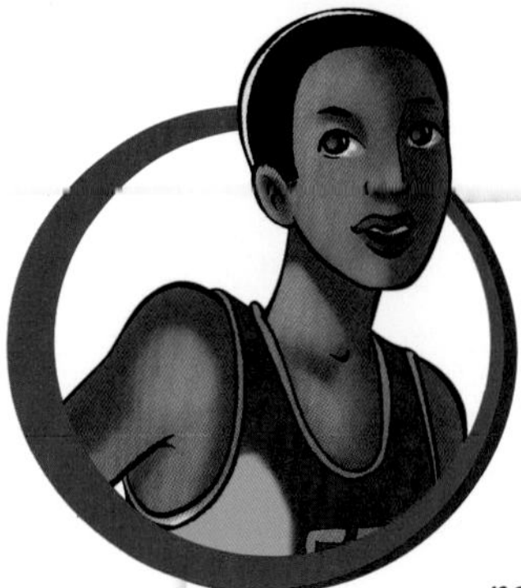

"Freaky Frank" Phillips earned his nickname because of his uncanny ability to use his "extra senses," a "gift" he inherited from his grandma. Though this eighth grader can't predict the winners of the next SUPERBOWL (or, he admits, "anything really useful"), Frank "knows" when someone is lying or otherwise up to no good. He gets "warnings" before trouble strikes. And sometimes he "sees things that aren't there"—at least to those less sensitive to things like auras and ghosts. Frank isn't sure what he wants to be when he grows up. He enjoys keeping tropical fish and does well in every subject, except math. "Numbers make my head hurt," Frank confesses. Frank spends lots of time with his family and his fish, but he's always up for an adventure with his friends.

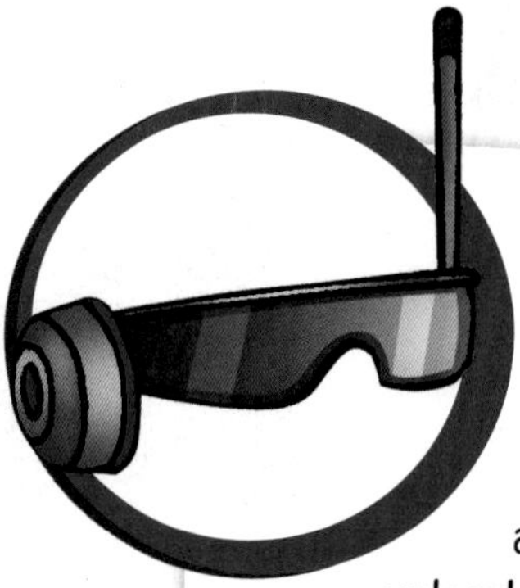

The Virtual Visors allow Einstein, Frank, Clarita, and Tracy to pursue their taste for adventure well beyond the boundaries of the bakery. Thanks to Einstein's brilliant software, the visors can simulate all kinds of locations and experiences based on the uploaded facts. Once inside the program, the visors become invisible. When danger gets too intense, the kids can always touch their Virtual Visors to return to the bakery. Sometimes the kids explore in the real world without the visors. But more often they use these devices to explore the mysteries and phenomena that intrigue each member of the group. The Virtual Visors are the ultimate virtual reality research tool, even though you never know what quirky things might happen thanks to Einstein's "Random Adventure Program."

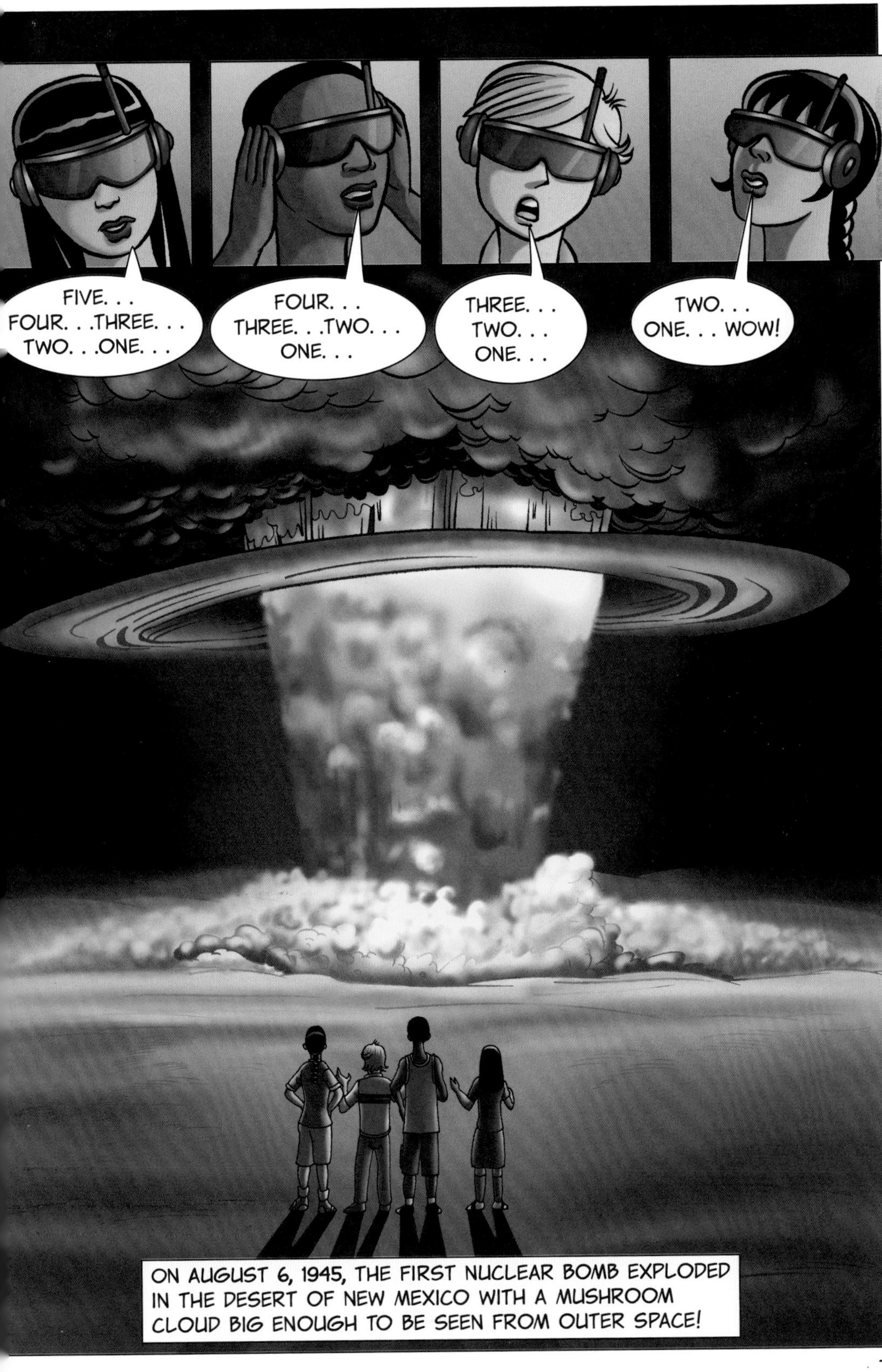
FIVE. . . FOUR. . .THREE. . . TWO. . .ONE. . .
FOUR. . . THREE. . .TWO. . . ONE. . .
THREE. . . TWO. . . ONE. . .
TWO. . . ONE. . . WOW!
ON AUGUST 6, 1945, THE FIRST NUCLEAR BOMB EXPLODED IN THE DESERT OF NEW MEXICO WITH A MUSHROOM CLOUD BIG ENOUGH TO BE SEEN FROM OUTER SPACE!

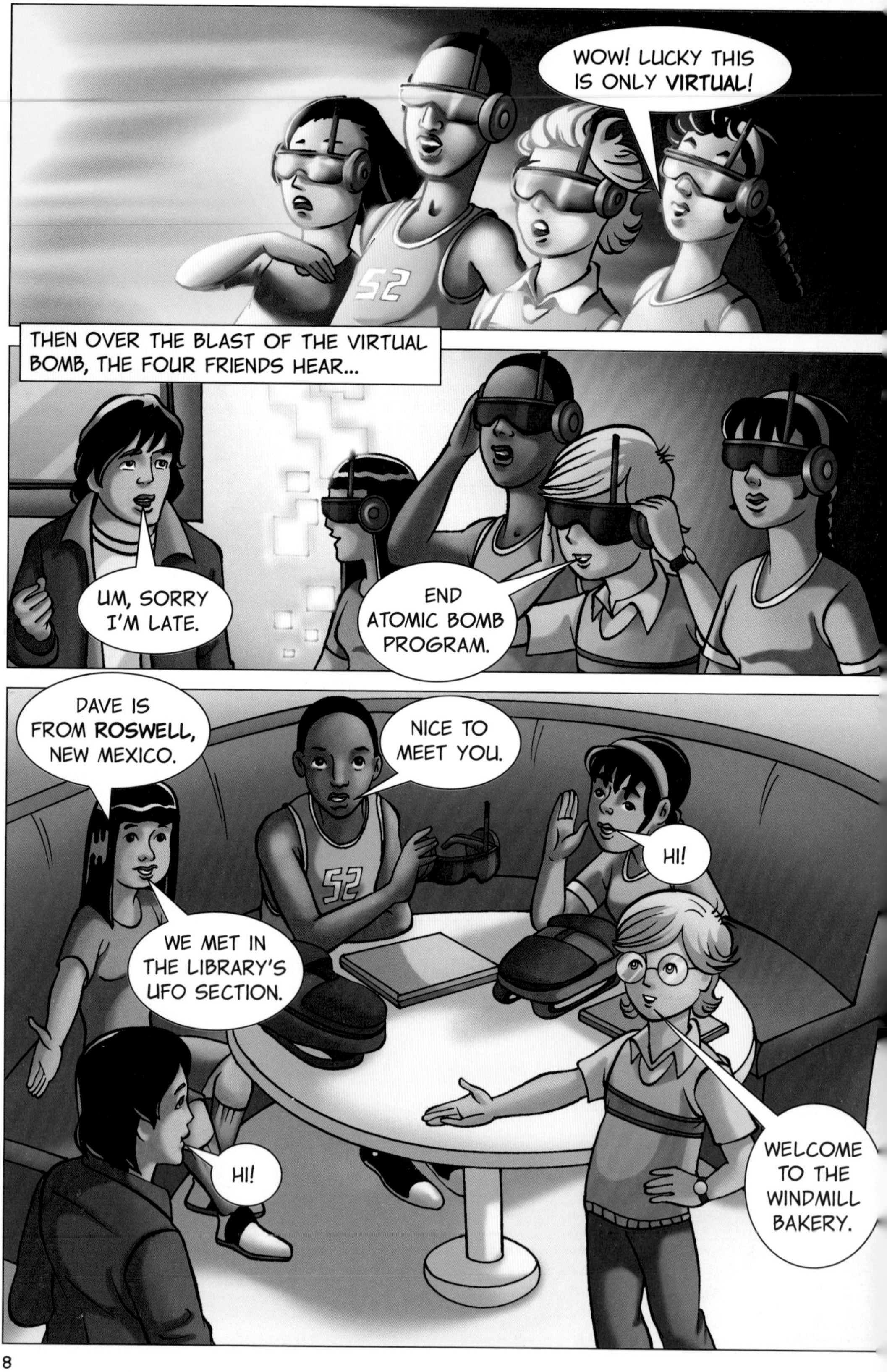
WOW! LUCKY THIS IS ONLY **VIRTUAL**!
THEN OVER THE BLAST OF THE VIRTUAL BOMB, THE FOUR FRIENDS HEAR...
UM, SORRY I'M LATE.
END ATOMIC BOMB PROGRAM.
DAVE IS FROM **ROSWELL**, NEW MEXICO.
NICE TO MEET YOU.
HI!
WE MET IN THE LIBRARY'S UFO SECTION.
HI!
WELCOME TO THE WINDMILL BAKERY.

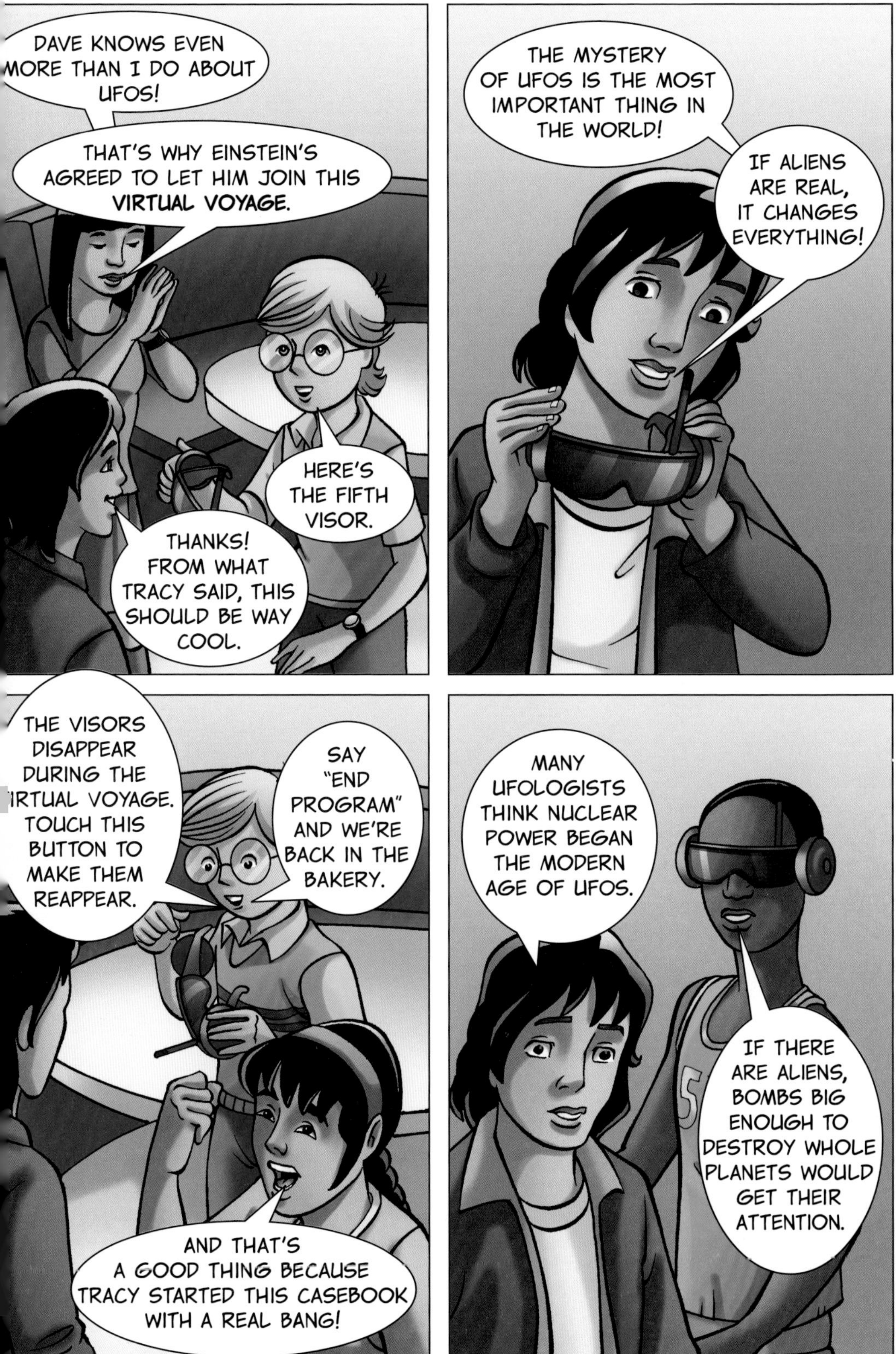
DAVE KNOWS EVEN MORE THAN I DO ABOUT UFOS!
THAT'S WHY EINSTEIN'S AGREED TO LET HIM JOIN THIS **VIRTUAL VOYAGE.**
HERE'S THE FIFTH VISOR.
THANKS! FROM WHAT TRACY SAID, THIS SHOULD BE WAY COOL.
THE MYSTERY OF UFOS IS THE MOST IMPORTANT THING IN THE WORLD!
IF ALIENS ARE REAL, IT CHANGES EVERYTHING!
THE VISORS DISAPPEAR DURING THE IRTUAL VOYAGE. TOUCH THIS BUTTON TO MAKE THEM REAPPEAR.
SAY "END PROGRAM" AND WE'RE BACK IN THE BAKERY.
AND THAT'S A GOOD THING BECAUSE TRACY STARTED THIS CASEBOOK WITH A REAL BANG!
MANY UFOLOGISTS THINK NUCLEAR POWER BEGAN THE MODERN AGE OF UFOS.
IF THERE ARE ALIENS, BOMBS BIG ENOUGH TO DESTROY WHOLE PLANETS WOULD GET THEIR ATTENTION.

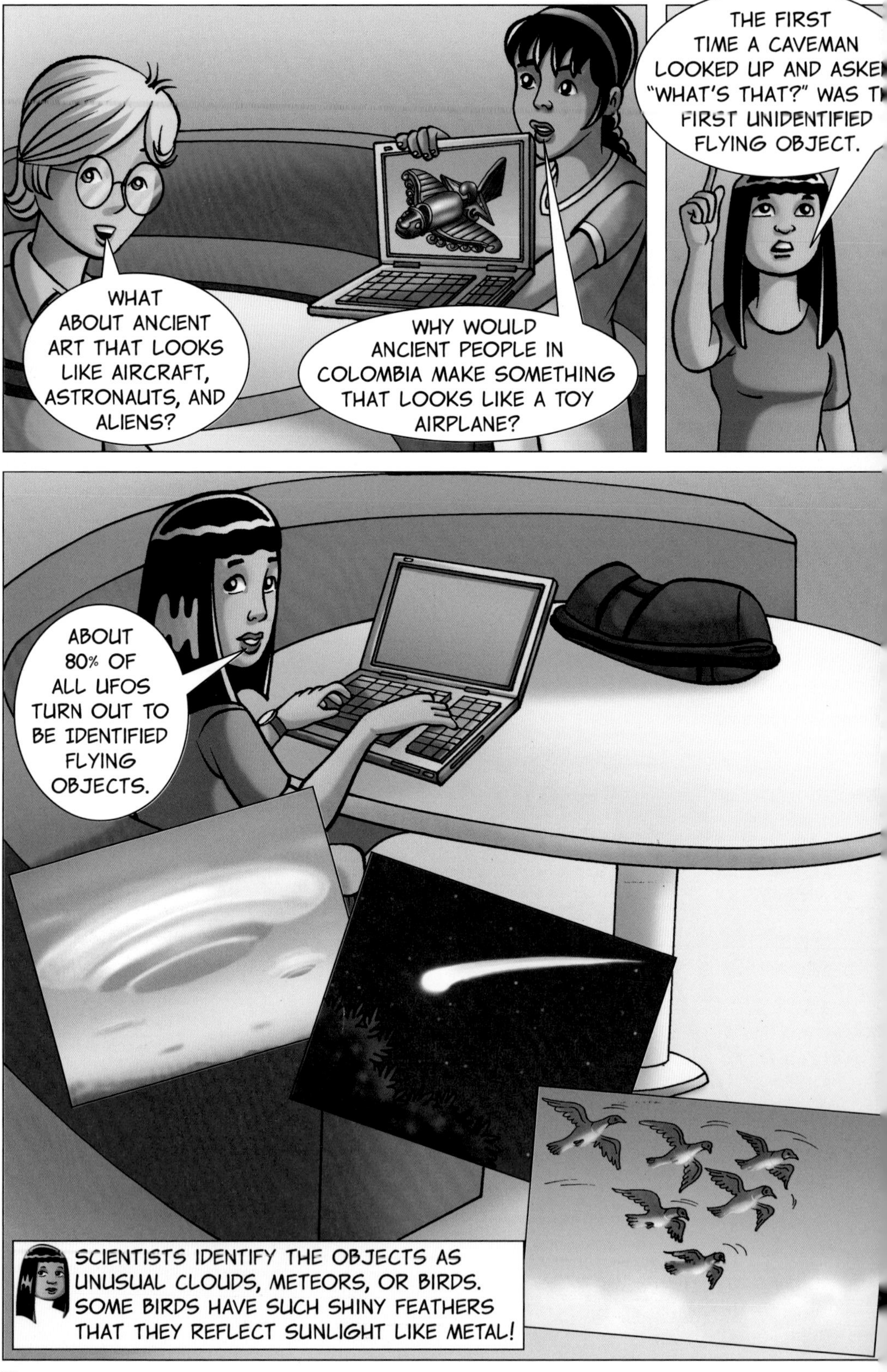
WHAT ABOUT ANCIENT ART THAT LOOKS LIKE AIRCRAFT, ASTRONAUTS, AND ALIENS?
WHY WOULD ANCIENT PEOPLE IN COLOMBIA MAKE SOMETHING THAT LOOKS LIKE A TOY AIRPLANE?
THE FIRST TIME A CAVEMAN LOOKED UP AND ASKE "WHAT'S THAT?" WAS T FIRST UNIDENTIFIED FLYING OBJECT.
ABOUT 80% OF ALL UFOS TURN OUT TO BE IDENTIFIED FLYING OBJECTS.
SCIENTISTS IDENTIFY THE OBJECTS AS UNUSUAL CLOUDS, METEORS, OR BIRDS. SOME BIRDS HAVE SUCH SHINY FEATHERS THAT THEY REFLECT SUNLIGHT LIKE METAL!

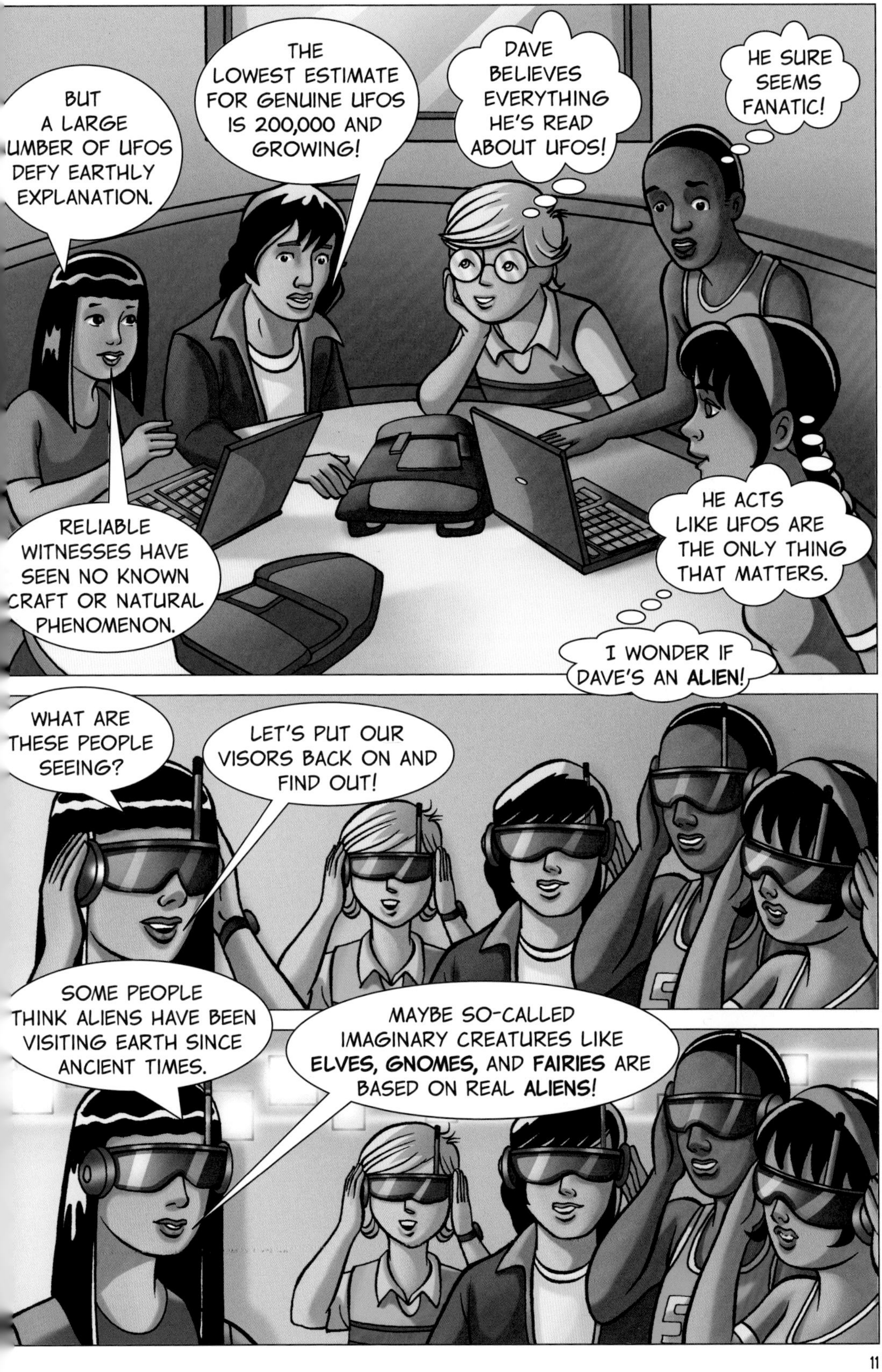
BUT A LARGE UMBER OF UFOS DEFY EARTHLY EXPLANATION.
THE LOWEST ESTIMATE FOR GENUINE UFOS IS 200,000 AND GROWING!
DAVE BELIEVES EVERYTHING HE'S READ ABOUT UFOS!
HE SURE SEEMS FANATIC!
RELIABLE WITNESSES HAVE SEEN NO KNOWN CRAFT OR NATURAL PHENOMENON.
HE ACTS LIKE UFOS ARE THE ONLY THING THAT MATTERS.
I WONDER IF DAVE'S AN **ALIEN**!
WHAT ARE THESE PEOPLE SEEING?
LET'S PUT OUR VISORS BACK ON AND FIND OUT!
SOME PEOPLE THINK ALIENS HAVE BEEN VISITING EARTH SINCE ANCIENT TIMES.
MAYBE SO-CALLED IMAGINARY CREATURES LIKE **ELVES, GNOMES,** AND **FAIRIES** ARE BASED ON REAL **ALIENS**!

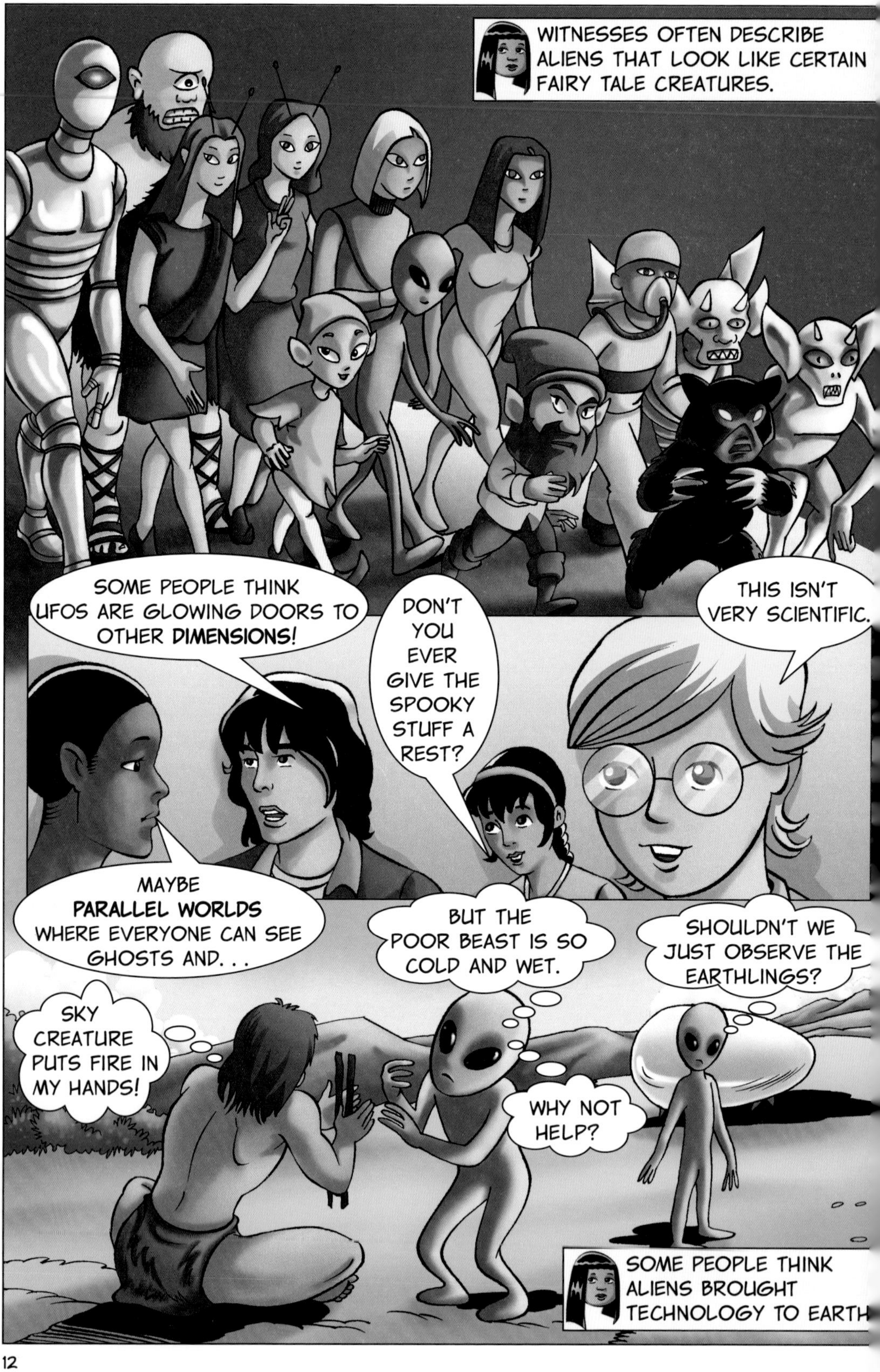

WITNESSES OFTEN DESCRIBE ALIENS THAT LOOK LIKE CERTAIN FAIRY TALE CREATURES.
SOME PEOPLE THINK UFOS ARE GLOWING DOORS TO OTHER DIMENSIONS!
DON'T YOU EVER GIVE THE SPOOKY STUFF A REST?
THIS ISN'T VERY SCIENTIFIC.
MAYBE PARALLEL WORLDS WHERE EVERYONE CAN SEE GHOSTS AND. . .
BUT THE POOR BEAST IS SO COLD AND WET.
SHOULDN'T WE JUST OBSERVE THE EARTHLINGS?
SKY CREATURE PUTS FIRE IN MY HANDS!
WHY NOT HELP?
SOME PEOPLE THINK ALIENS BROUGHT TECHNOLOGY TO EARTH

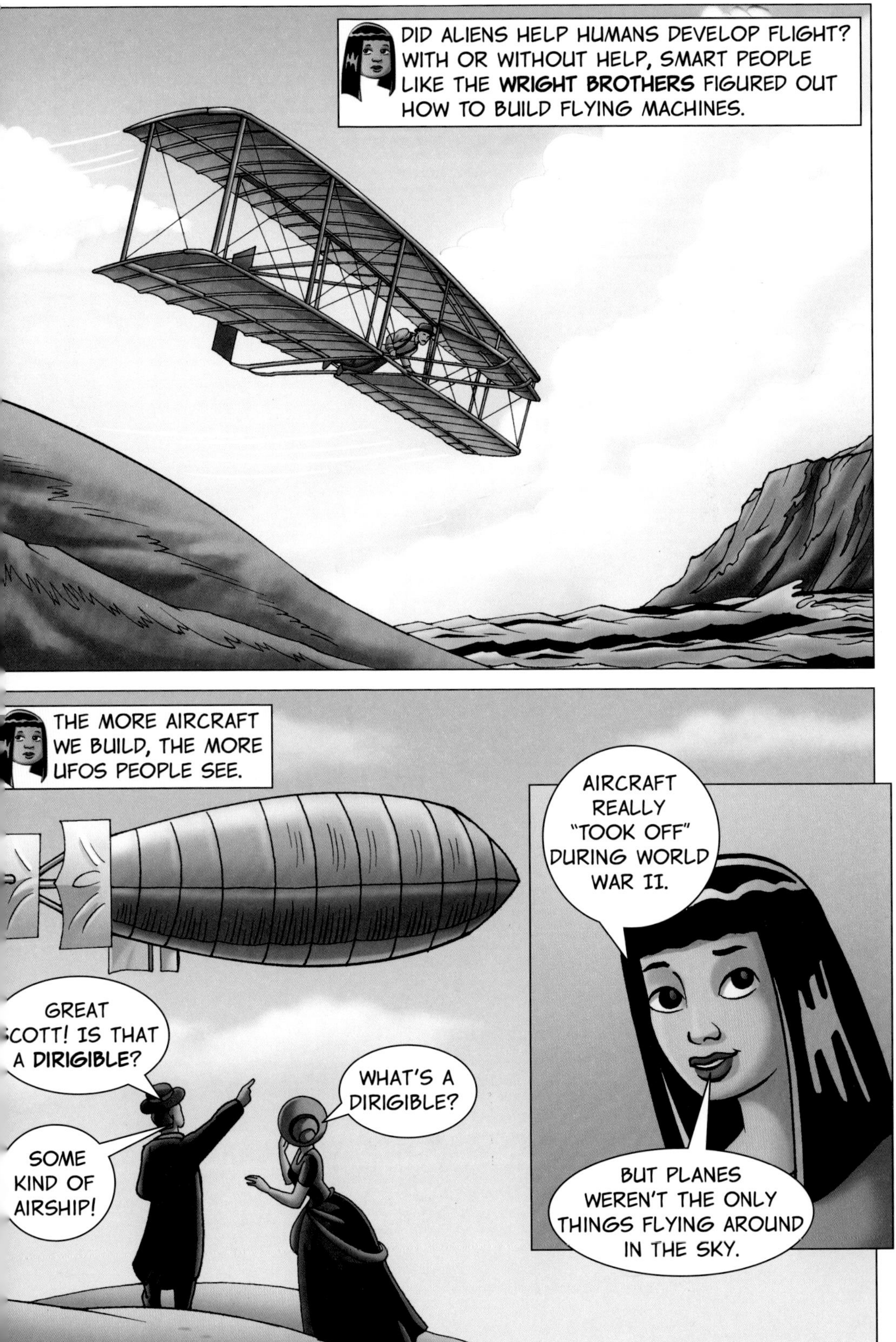
DID ALIENS HELP HUMANS DEVELOP FLIGHT? WITH OR WITHOUT HELP, SMART PEOPLE LIKE THE **WRIGHT BROTHERS** FIGURED OUT HOW TO BUILD FLYING MACHINES.
THE MORE AIRCRAFT WE BUILD, THE MORE UFOS PEOPLE SEE.
GREAT SCOTT! IS THAT A **DIRIGIBLE**?
WHAT'S A DIRIGIBLE?
SOME KIND OF AIRSHIP!
AIRCRAFT REALLY "TOOK OFF" DURING WORLD WAR II.
BUT PLANES WEREN'T THE ONLY THINGS FLYING AROUND IN THE SKY.

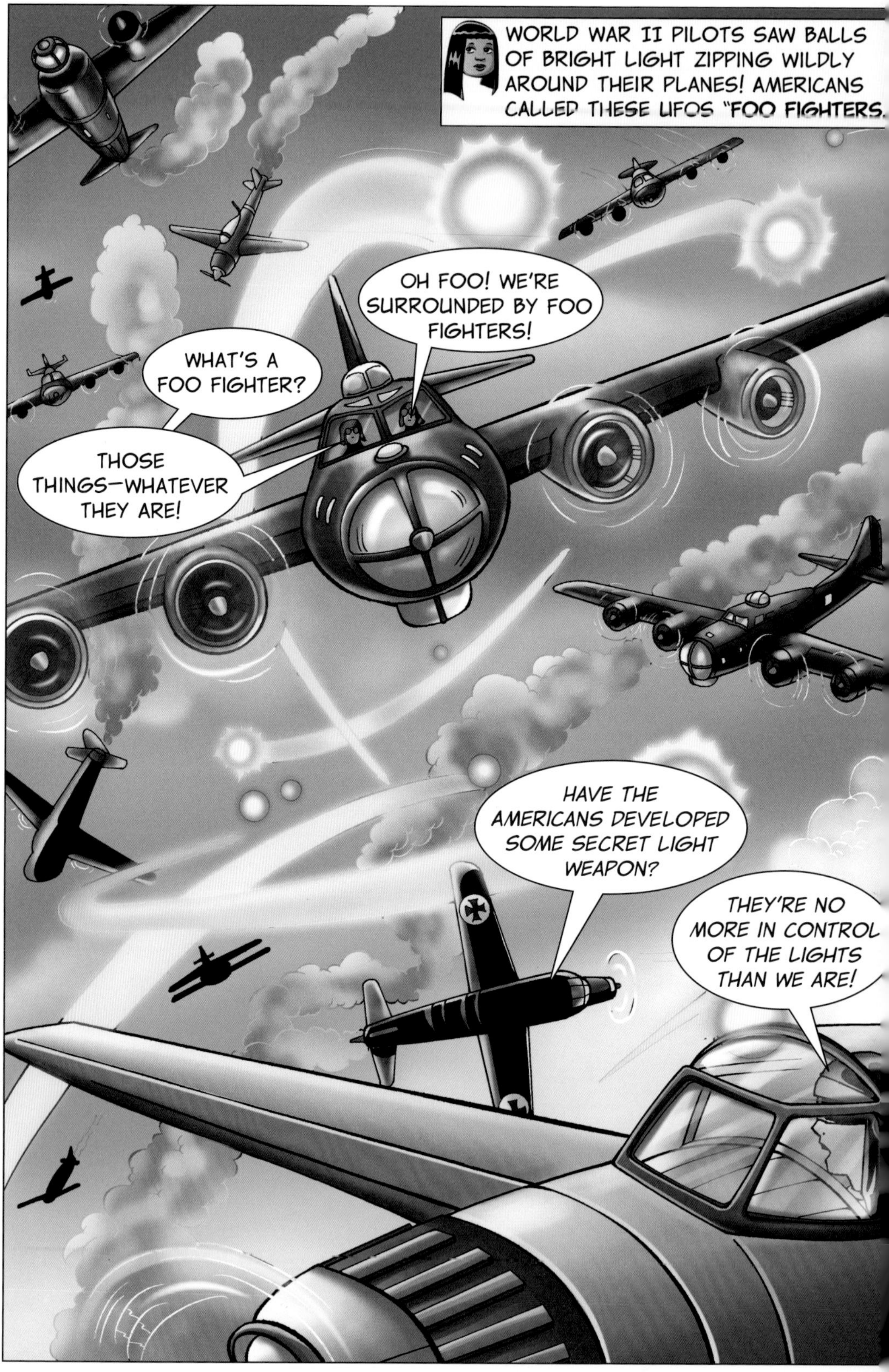
WORLD WAR II PILOTS SAW BALLS OF BRIGHT LIGHT ZIPPING WILDLY AROUND THEIR PLANES! AMERICANS CALLED THESE UFOS "FOO FIGHTERS.
OH FOO! WE'RE SURROUNDED BY FOO FIGHTERS!
WHAT'S A FOO FIGHTER?
THOSE THINGS—WHATEVER THEY ARE!
HAVE THE AMERICANS DEVELOPED SOME SECRET LIGHT WEAPON?
THEY'RE NO MORE IN CONTROL OF THE LIGHTS THAN WE ARE!

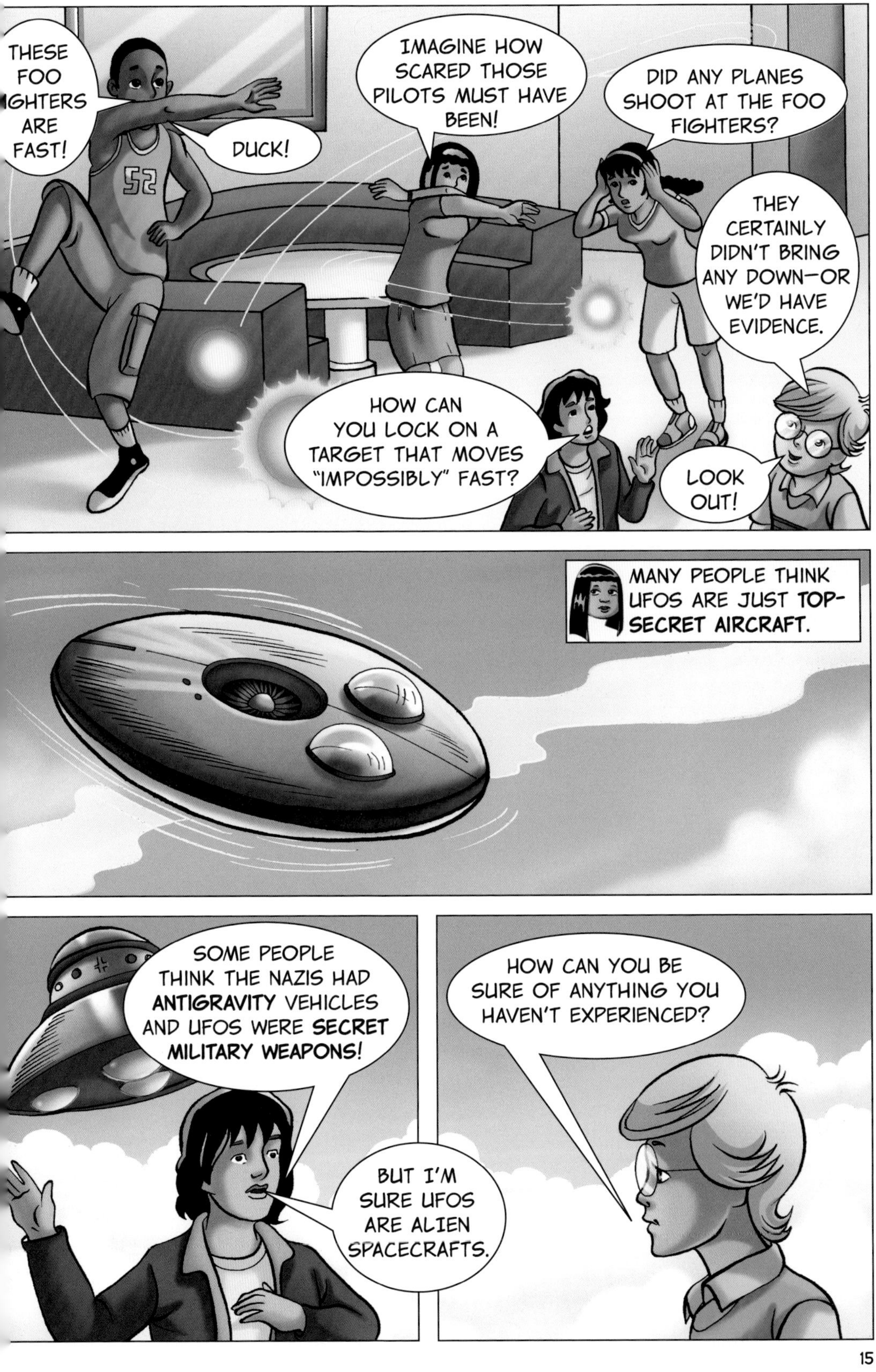
THESE FOO IGHTERS ARE FAST!
DUCK!
IMAGINE HOW SCARED THOSE PILOTS MUST HAVE BEEN!
DID ANY PLANES SHOOT AT THE FOO FIGHTERS?
THEY CERTAINLY DIDN'T BRING ANY DOWN—OR WE'D HAVE EVIDENCE.
HOW CAN YOU LOCK ON A TARGET THAT MOVES "IMPOSSIBLY" FAST?
LOOK OUT!
MANY PEOPLE THINK UFOS ARE JUST **TOP-SECRET AIRCRAFT**.
SOME PEOPLE THINK THE NAZIS HAD **ANTIGRAVITY** VEHICLES AND UFOS WERE **SECRET MILITARY WEAPONS**!
BUT I'M SURE UFOS ARE ALIEN SPACECRAFTS.
HOW CAN YOU BE SURE OF ANYTHING YOU HAVEN'T EXPERIENCED?

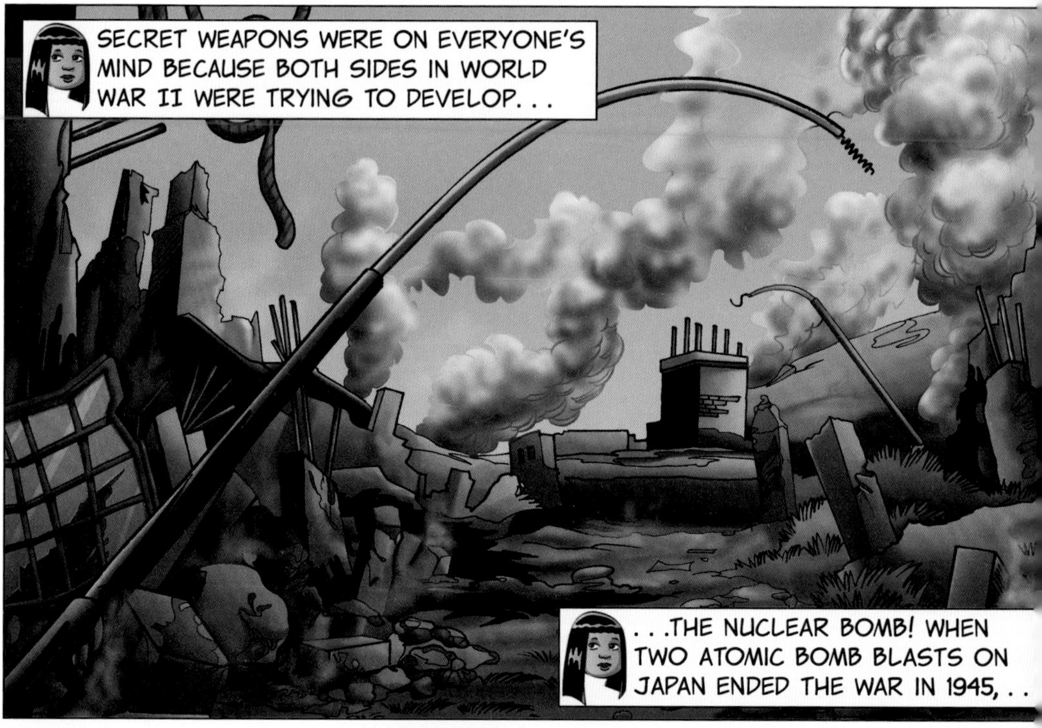
SECRET WEAPONS WERE ON EVERYONE'S MIND BECAUSE BOTH SIDES IN WORLD WAR II WERE TRYING TO DEVELOP. . .
. . .THE NUCLEAR BOMB! WHEN TWO ATOMIC BOMB BLASTS ON JAPAN ENDED THE WAR IN 1945, . .

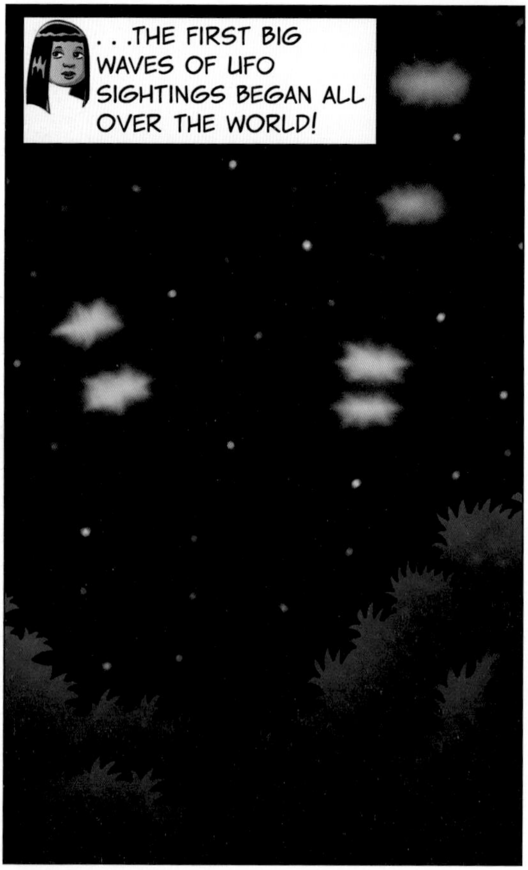
. . .THE FIRST BIG WAVES OF UFO SIGHTINGS BEGAN ALL OVER THE WORLD!

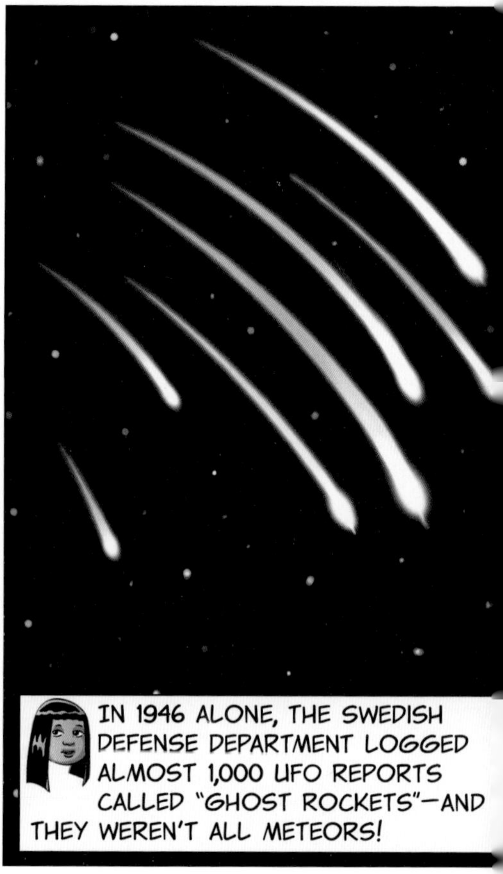
IN 1946 ALONE, THE SWEDISH DEFENSE DEPARTMENT LOGGED ALMOST 1,000 UFO REPORTS CALLED "GHOST ROCKETS"—AND THEY WEREN'T ALL METEORS!

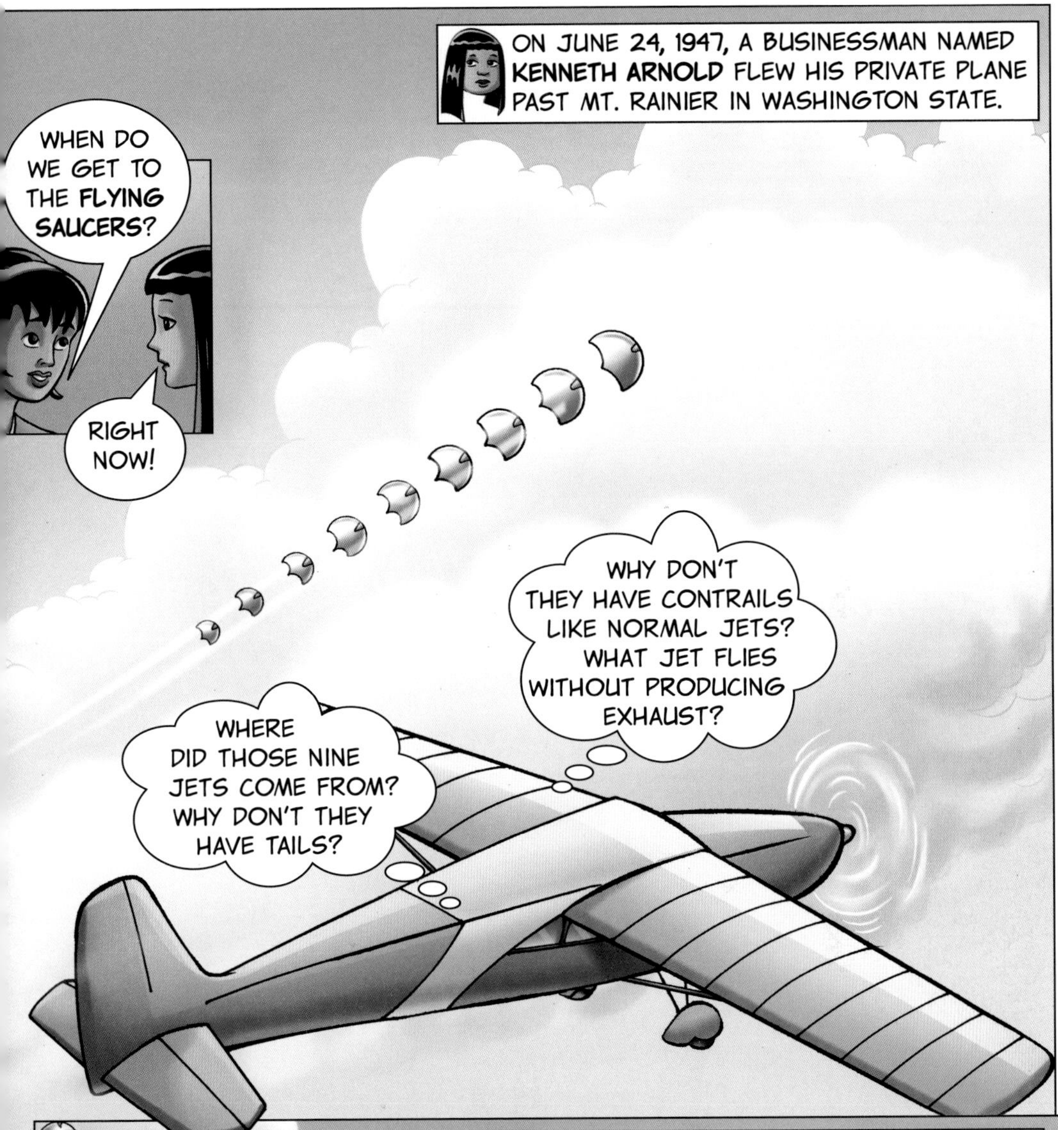
ON JUNE 24, 1947, A BUSINESSMAN NAMED KENNETH ARNOLD FLEW HIS PRIVATE PLANE PAST MT. RAINIER IN WASHINGTON STATE.
WHEN DO WE GET TO THE FLYING SAUCERS?
RIGHT NOW!
WHY DON'T THEY HAVE CONTRAILS LIKE NORMAL JETS? WHAT JET FLIES WITHOUT PRODUCING EXHAUST?
WHERE DID THOSE NINE JETS COME FROM? WHY DON'T THEY HAVE TAILS?

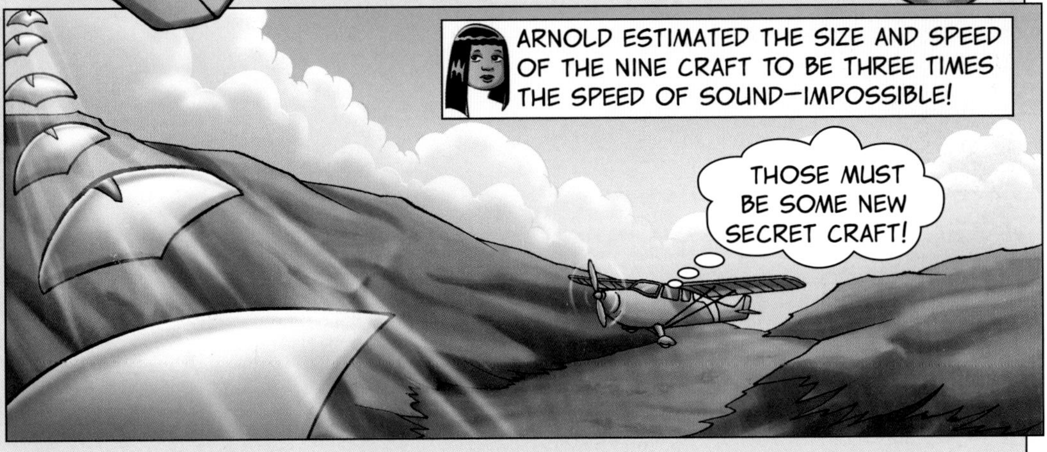
ARNOLD ESTIMATED THE SIZE AND SPEED OF THE NINE CRAFT TO BE THREE TIMES THE SPEED OF SOUND—IMPOSSIBLE!
THOSE MUST BE SOME NEW SECRET CRAFT!

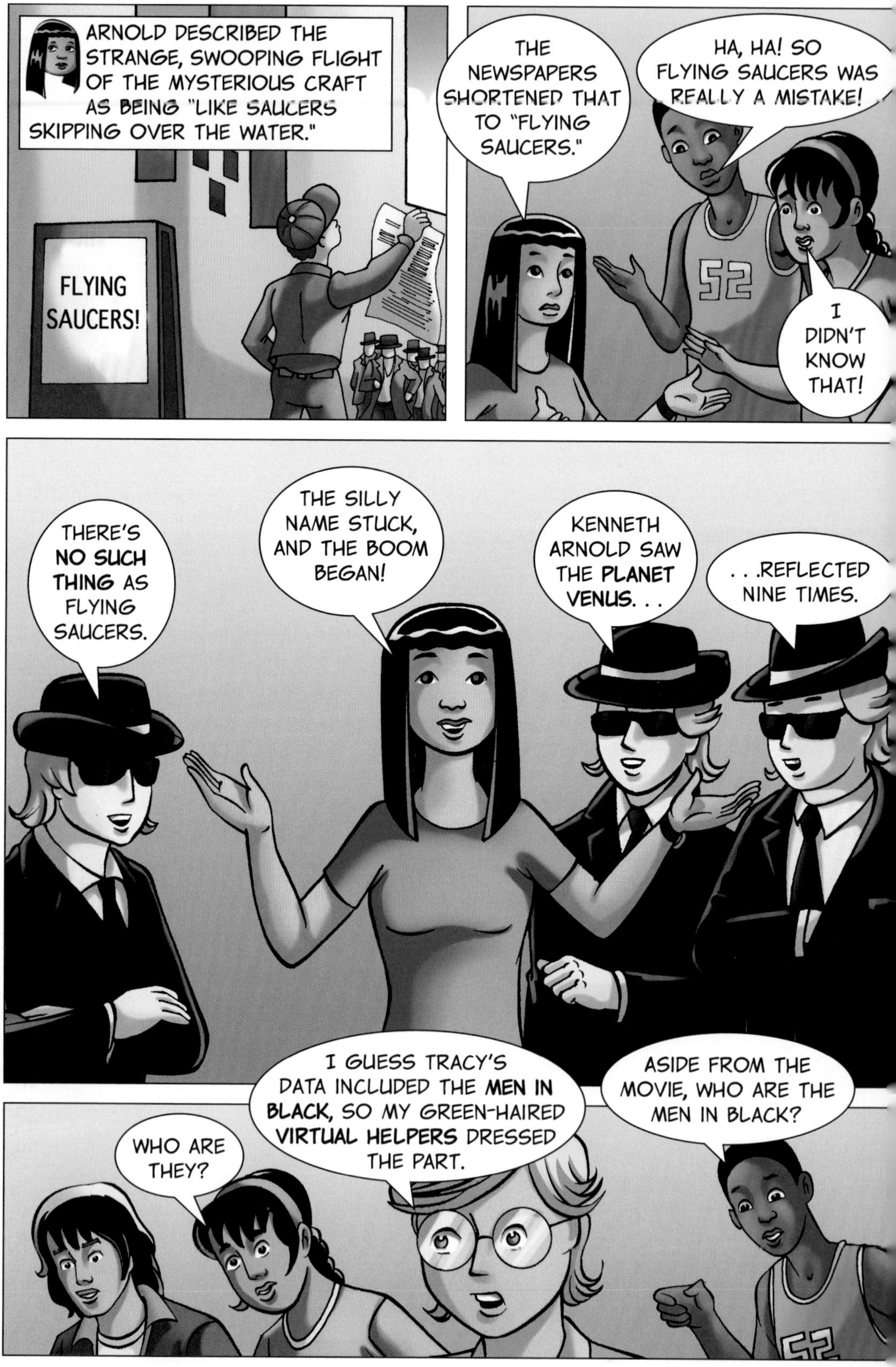
ARNOLD DESCRIBED THE STRANGE, SWOOPING FLIGHT OF THE MYSTERIOUS CRAFT AS BEING "LIKE SAUCERS SKIPPING OVER THE WATER."
FLYING SAUCERS!
THE NEWSPAPERS SHORTENED THAT TO "FLYING SAUCERS."
HA, HA! SO FLYING SAUCERS WAS REALLY A MISTAKE!
I DIDN'T KNOW THAT!
THERE'S **NO SUCH THING** AS FLYING SAUCERS.
THE SILLY NAME STUCK, AND THE BOOM BEGAN!
KENNETH ARNOLD SAW THE **PLANET VENUS**. . .
. . .REFLECTED NINE TIMES.
WHO ARE THEY?
I GUESS TRACY'S DATA INCLUDED THE **MEN IN BLACK**, SO MY GREEN-HAIRED **VIRTUAL HELPERS** DRESSED THE PART.
ASIDE FROM THE MOVIE, WHO ARE THE MEN IN BLACK?

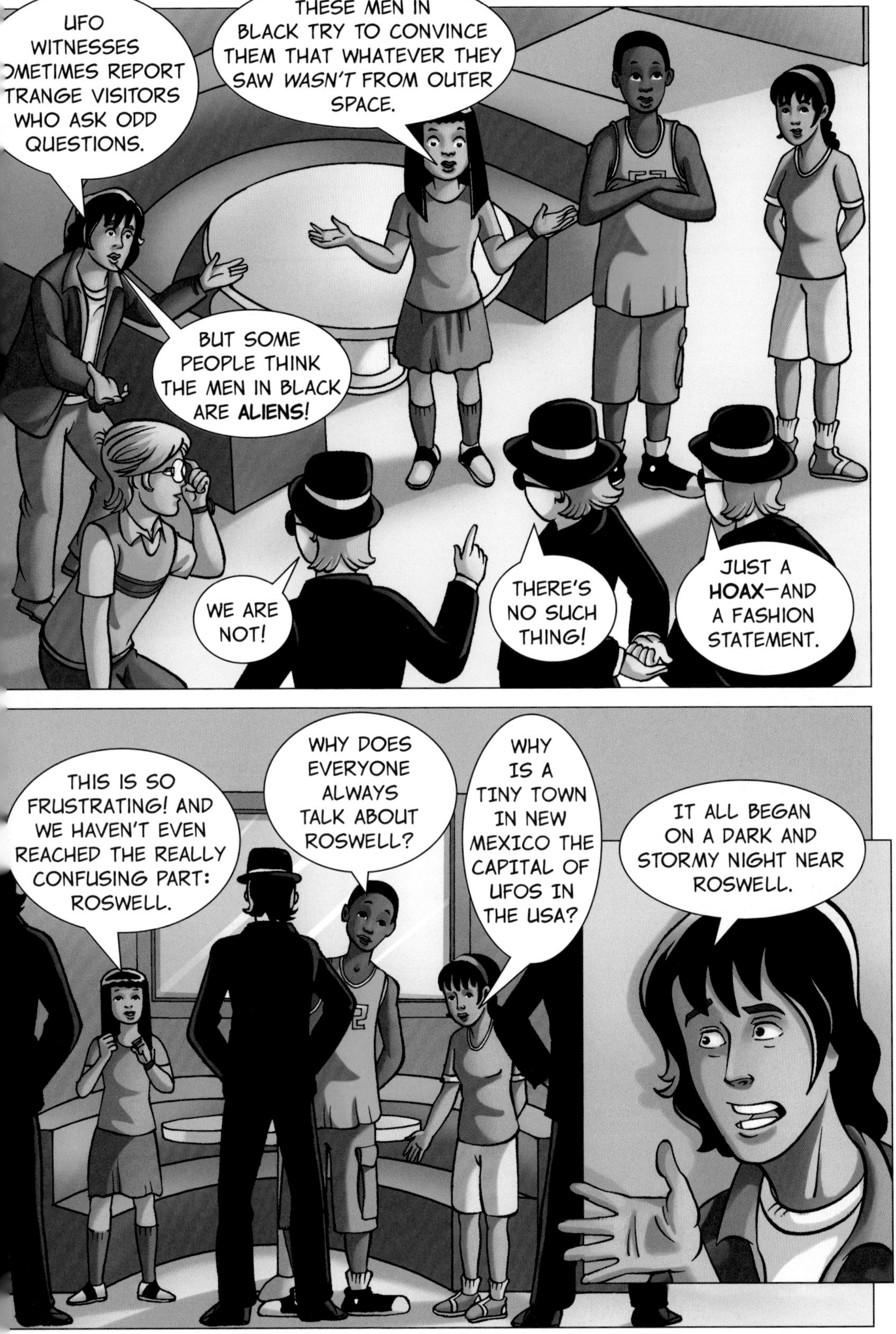
UFO WITNESSES OMETIMES REPORT TRANGE VISITORS WHO ASK ODD QUESTIONS.
THESE MEN IN BLACK TRY TO CONVINCE THEM THAT WHATEVER THEY SAW *WASN'T* FROM OUTER SPACE.
BUT SOME PEOPLE THINK THE MEN IN BLACK ARE **ALIENS**!
WE ARE NOT!
THERE'S NO SUCH THING!
JUST A **HOAX**—AND A FASHION STATEMENT.
THIS IS SO FRUSTRATING! AND WE HAVEN'T EVEN REACHED THE REALLY CONFUSING PART: ROSWELL.
WHY DOES EVERYONE ALWAYS TALK ABOUT ROSWELL?
WHY IS A TINY TOWN IN NEW MEXICO THE CAPITAL OF UFOS IN THE USA?
IT ALL BEGAN ON A DARK AND STORMY NIGHT NEAR ROSWELL.

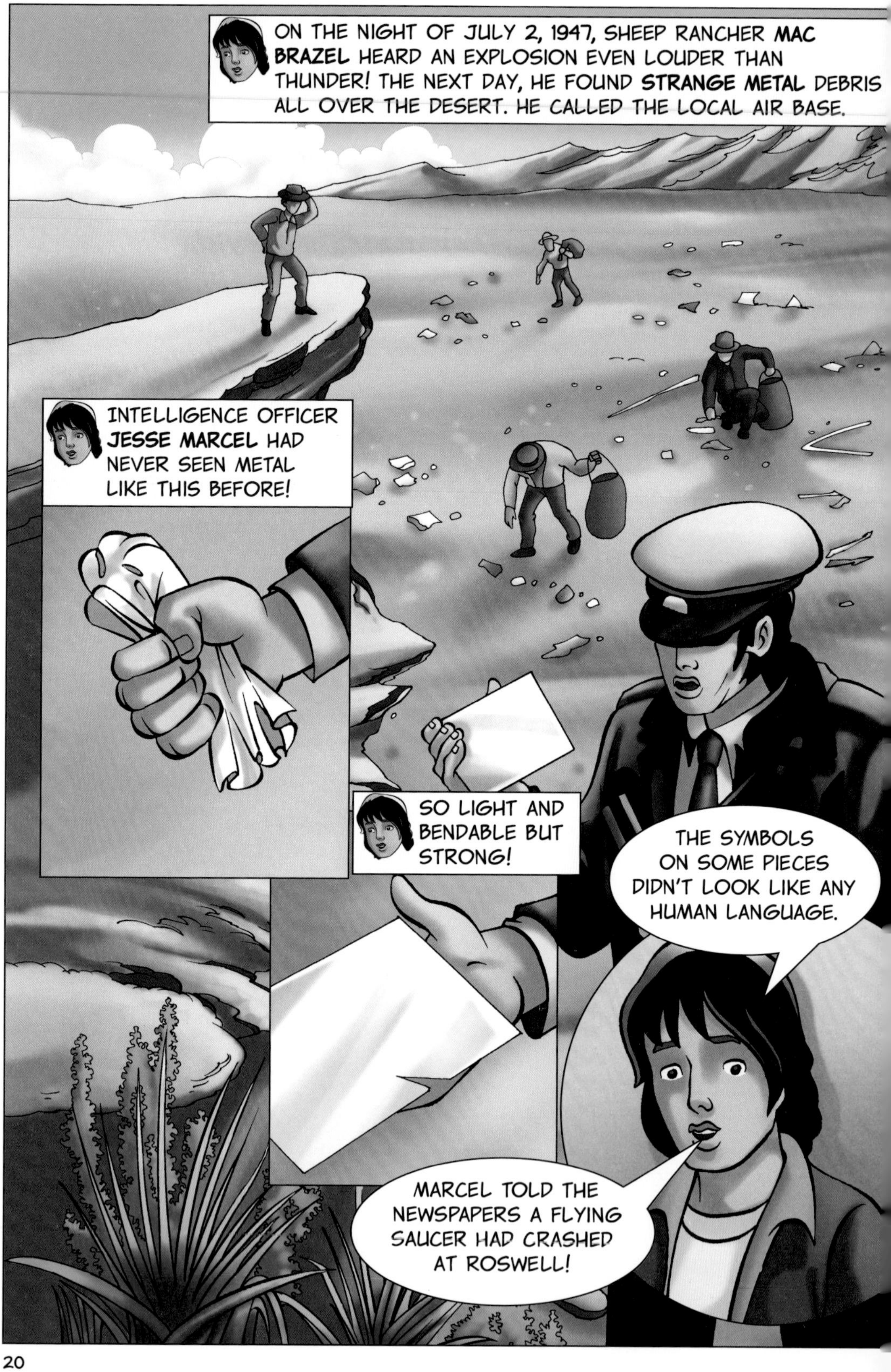
ON THE NIGHT OF JULY 2, 1947, SHEEP RANCHER MAC BRAZEL HEARD AN EXPLOSION EVEN LOUDER THAN THUNDER! THE NEXT DAY, HE FOUND STRANGE METAL DEBRIS ALL OVER THE DESERT. HE CALLED THE LOCAL AIR BASE.
INTELLIGENCE OFFICER JESSE MARCEL HAD NEVER SEEN METAL LIKE THIS BEFORE!
SO LIGHT AND BENDABLE BUT STRONG!
THE SYMBOLS ON SOME PIECES DIDN'T LOOK LIKE ANY HUMAN LANGUAGE.
MARCEL TOLD THE NEWSPAPERS A FLYING SAUCER HAD CRASHED AT ROSWELL!

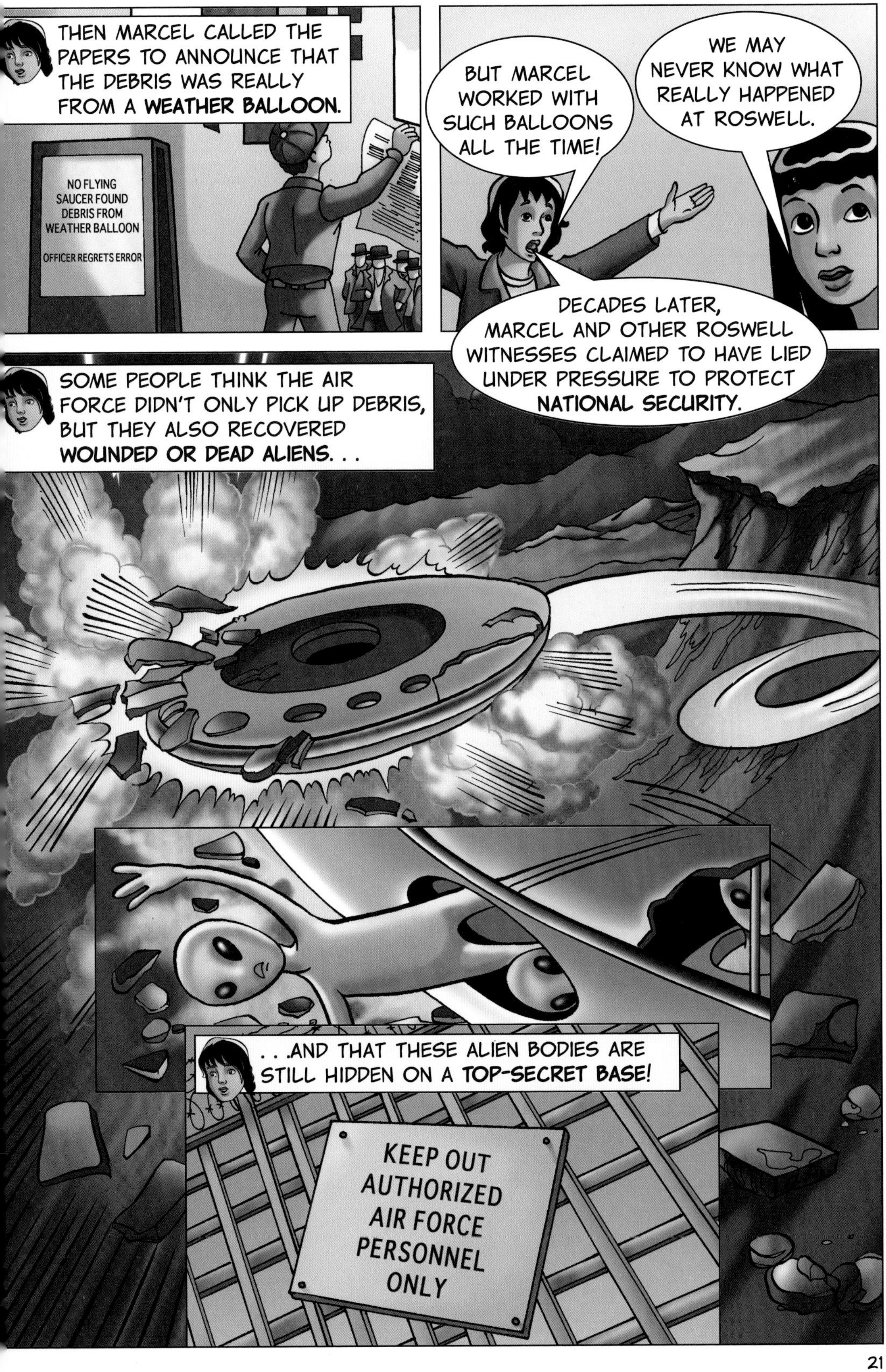
THEN MARCEL CALLED THE PAPERS TO ANNOUNCE THAT THE DEBRIS WAS REALLY FROM A **WEATHER BALLOON**.
NO FLYING SAUCER FOUND DEBRIS FROM WEATHER BALLOON
OFFICER REGRETS ERROR
BUT MARCEL WORKED WITH SUCH BALLOONS ALL THE TIME!
WE MAY NEVER KNOW WHAT REALLY HAPPENED AT ROSWELL.
DECADES LATER, MARCEL AND OTHER ROSWELL WITNESSES CLAIMED TO HAVE LIED UNDER PRESSURE TO PROTECT **NATIONAL SECURITY**.
SOME PEOPLE THINK THE AIR FORCE DIDN'T ONLY PICK UP DEBRIS, BUT THEY ALSO RECOVERED **WOUNDED OR DEAD ALIENS**. . .
. . .AND THAT THESE ALIEN BODIES ARE STILL HIDDEN ON A **TOP-SECRET BASE**!
KEEP OUT AUTHORIZED AIR FORCE PERSONNEL ONLY

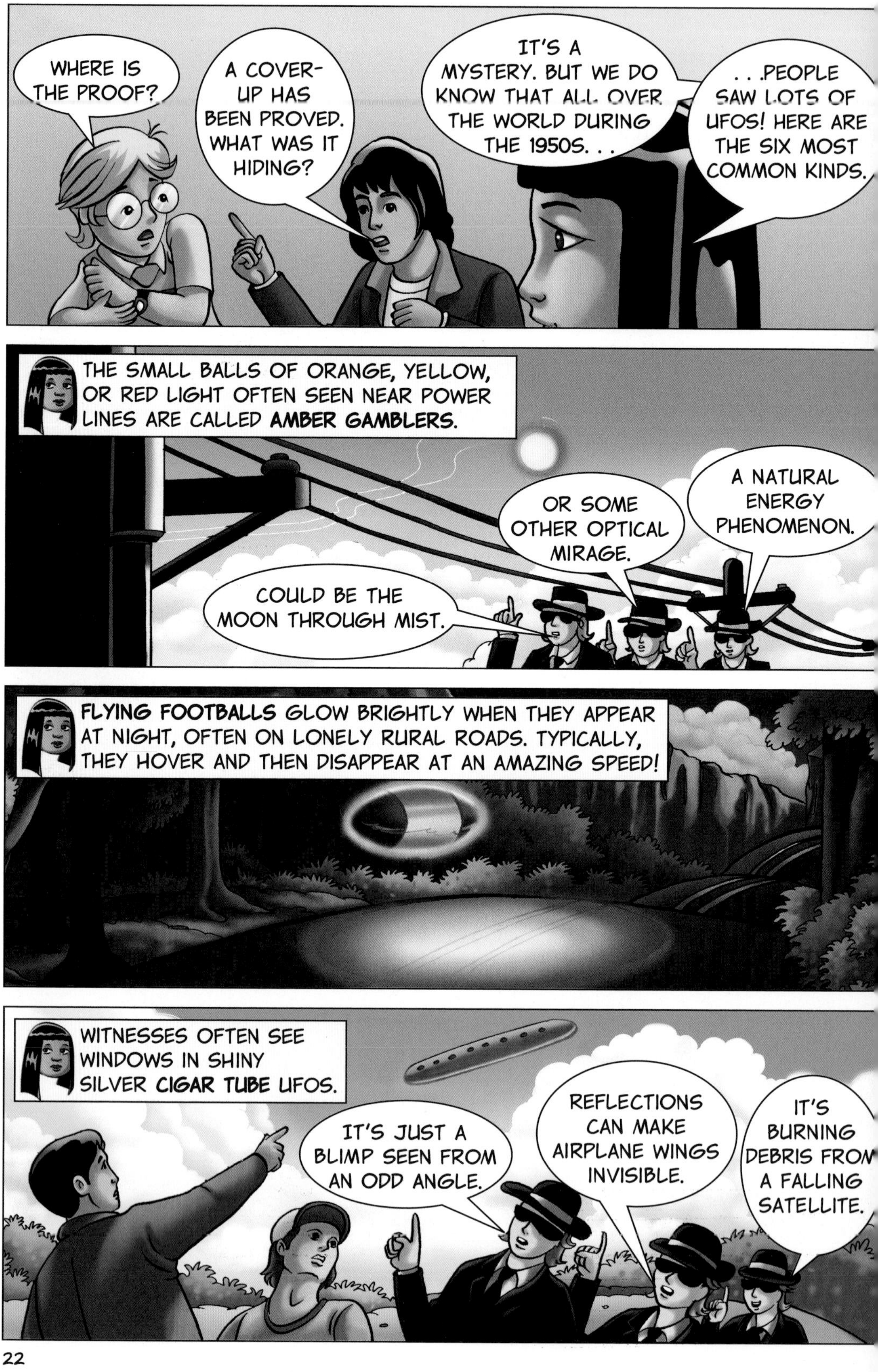
WHERE IS THE PROOF?
A COVER-UP HAS BEEN PROVED. WHAT WAS IT HIDING?
IT'S A MYSTERY. BUT WE DO KNOW THAT ALL OVER THE WORLD DURING THE 1950S. . .
. . .PEOPLE SAW LOTS OF UFOS! HERE ARE THE SIX MOST COMMON KINDS.
THE SMALL BALLS OF ORANGE, YELLOW, OR RED LIGHT OFTEN SEEN NEAR POWER LINES ARE CALLED **AMBER GAMBLERS**.
COULD BE THE MOON THROUGH MIST.
OR SOME OTHER OPTICAL MIRAGE.
A NATURAL ENERGY PHENOMENON.
FLYING FOOTBALLS GLOW BRIGHTLY WHEN THEY APPEAR AT NIGHT, OFTEN ON LONELY RURAL ROADS. TYPICALLY, THEY HOVER AND THEN DISAPPEAR AT AN AMAZING SPEED!
WITNESSES OFTEN SEE WINDOWS IN SHINY SILVER **CIGAR TUBE** UFOS.
IT'S JUST A BLIMP SEEN FROM AN ODD ANGLE.
REFLECTIONS CAN MAKE AIRPLANE WINGS INVISIBLE.
IT'S BURNING DEBRIS FROM A FALLING SATELLITE.

COMMON IN THE 1950S, **UPTURNED PLATES** BECAME RARE AFTER THE '70S. IS UFO TECHNOLOGY ADVANCING OR DO DIFFERENT UFOS COME FROM DIFFERENT PLACES?

 AT NIGHT, **SATURN-SHAPED** UFOS GIVE OFF LIGHT FROM INSIDE, LIKE A HOUSE WHERE SOMEONE'S HOME.

 TRIANGULAR UFOS LOOK LIKE THREE LIGHTS FLYING IN FORMATION.

SOME AIRCRAFT CAN LOOK LIKE THIS. . .

. . WHEN VIEWED FROM CERTAIN ANGLES.

AIRCRAFT LIKE THE LOCKHEED TRISTAR HAVE **HIGH TAILLIGHTS.**

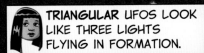

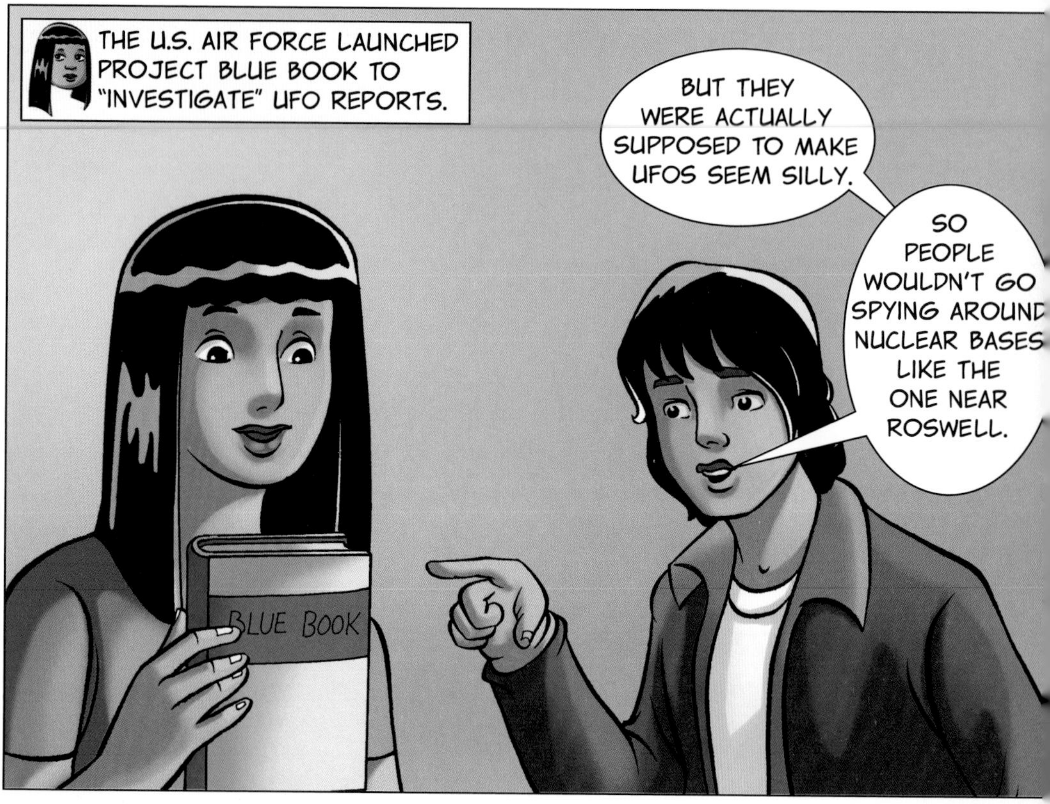
THE U.S. AIR FORCE LAUNCHED PROJECT BLUE BOOK TO "INVESTIGATE" UFO REPORTS.
BUT THEY WERE ACTUALLY SUPPOSED TO MAKE UFOS SEEM SILLY.
SO PEOPLE WOULDN'T GO SPYING AROUND NUCLEAR BASES LIKE THE ONE NEAR ROSWELL.
BLUE BOOK

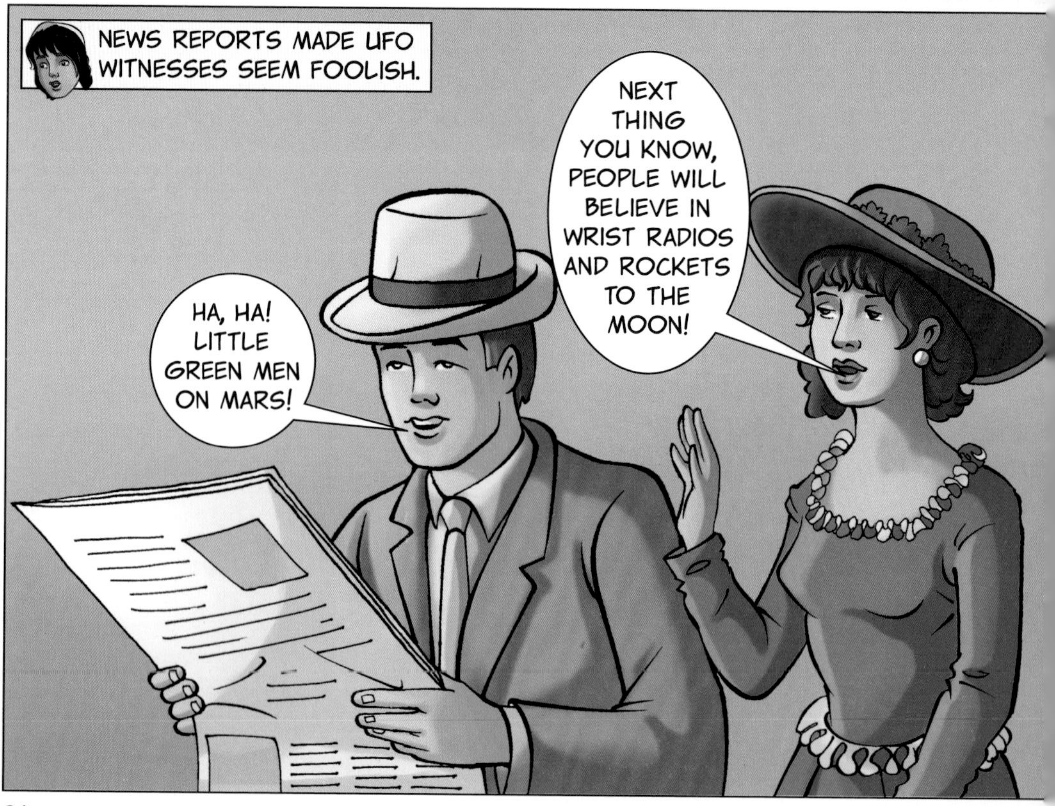
NEWS REPORTS MADE UFO WITNESSES SEEM FOOLISH.
HA, HA! LITTLE GREEN MEN ON MARS!
NEXT THING YOU KNOW, PEOPLE WILL BELIEVE IN WRIST RADIOS AND ROCKETS TO THE MOON!

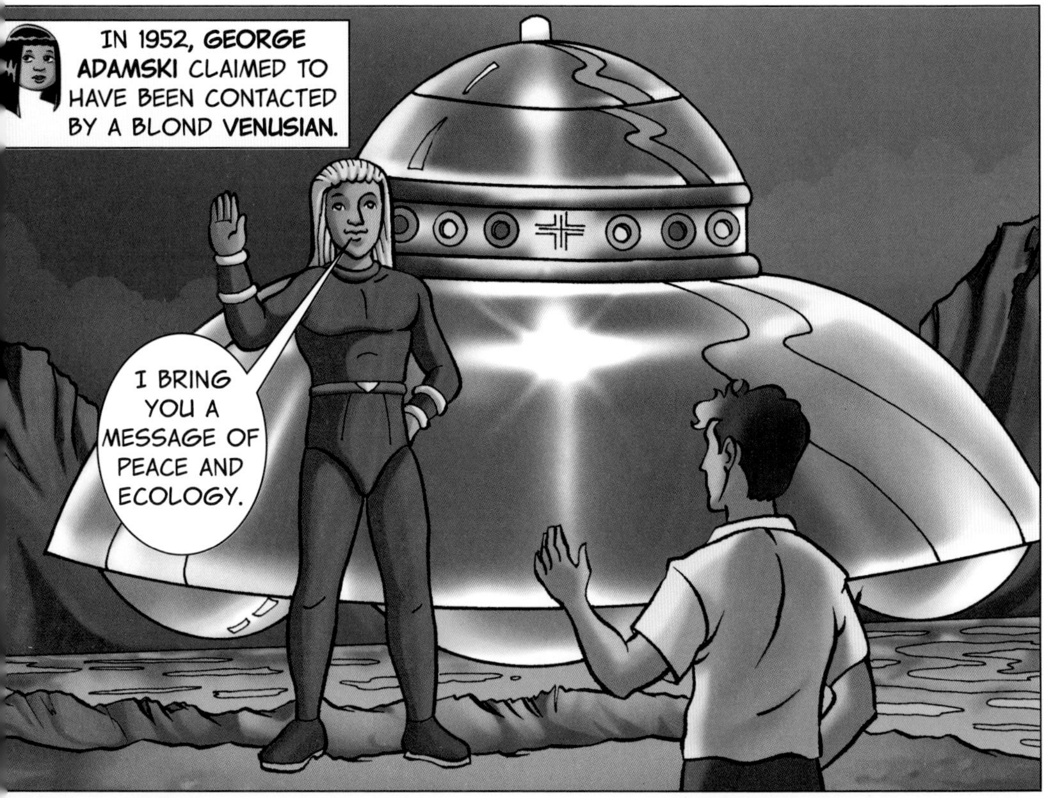
IN 1952, GEORGE ADAMSKI CLAIMED TO HAVE BEEN CONTACTED BY A BLOND VENUSIAN.
I BRING YOU A MESSAGE OF PEACE AND ECOLOGY.

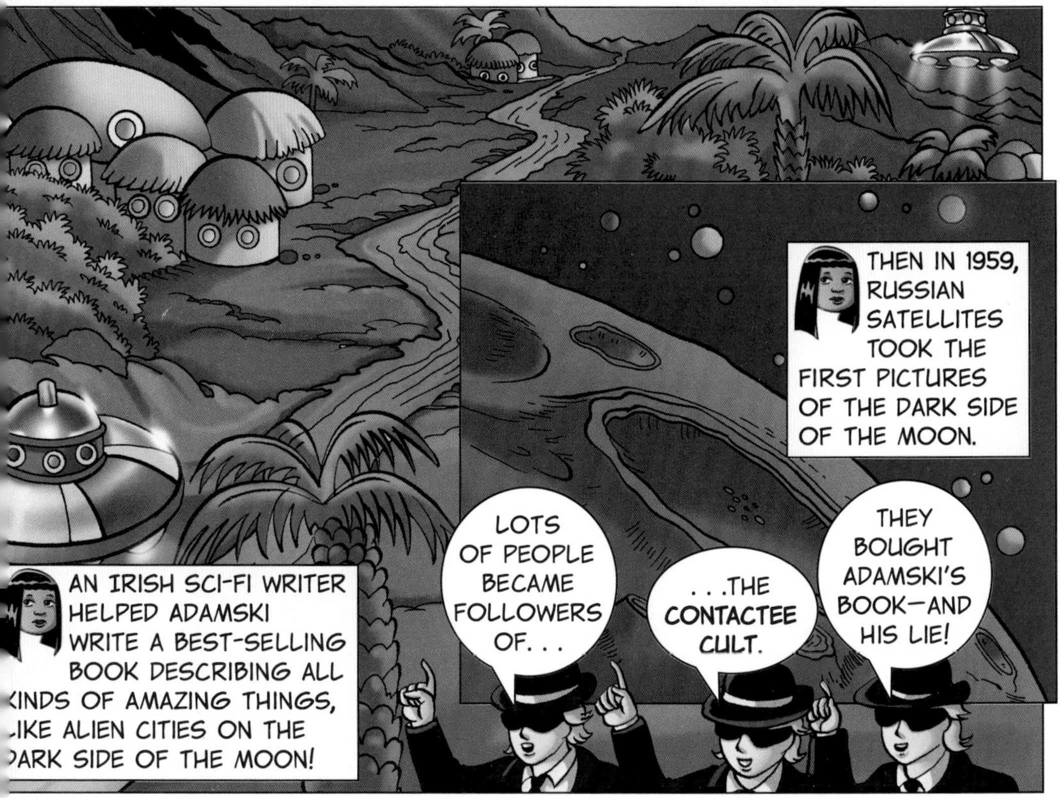
THEN IN 1959, RUSSIAN SATELLITES TOOK THE FIRST PICTURES OF THE DARK SIDE OF THE MOON.
AN IRISH SCI-FI WRITER HELPED ADAMSKI WRITE A BEST-SELLING BOOK DESCRIBING ALL KINDS OF AMAZING THINGS, LIKE ALIEN CITIES ON THE DARK SIDE OF THE MOON!
LOTS OF PEOPLE BECAME FOLLOWERS OF. . .
. . .THE CONTACTEE CULT.
THEY BOUGHT ADAMSKI'S BOOK—AND HIS LIE!

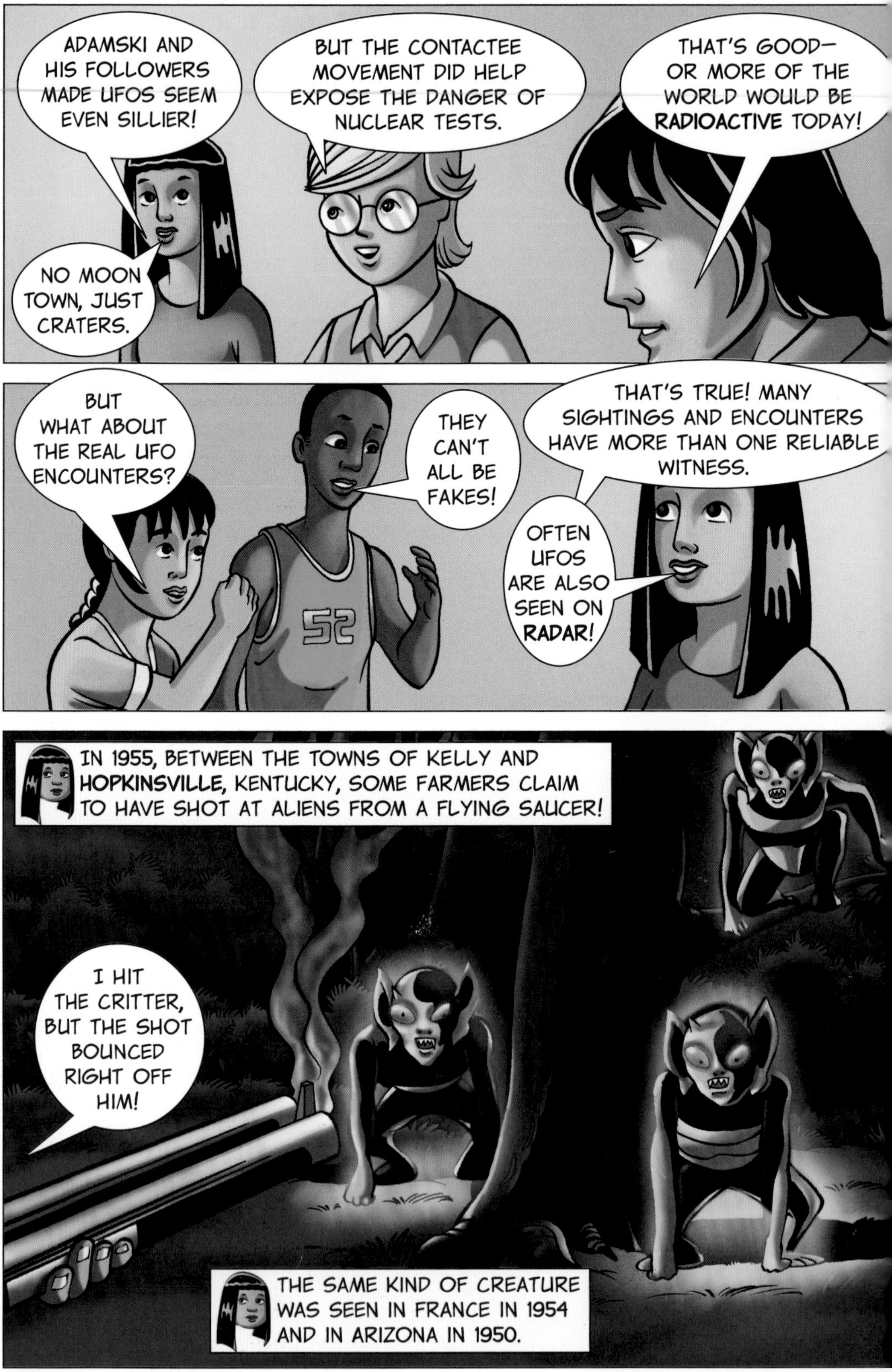

ADAMSKI AND HIS FOLLOWERS MADE UFOS SEEM EVEN SILLIER!
NO MOON TOWN, JUST CRATERS.
BUT THE CONTACTEE MOVEMENT DID HELP EXPOSE THE DANGER OF NUCLEAR TESTS.
THAT'S GOOD— OR MORE OF THE WORLD WOULD BE **RADIOACTIVE** TODAY!
BUT WHAT ABOUT THE REAL UFO ENCOUNTERS?
THEY CAN'T ALL BE FAKES!
THAT'S TRUE! MANY SIGHTINGS AND ENCOUNTERS HAVE MORE THAN ONE RELIABLE WITNESS.
OFTEN UFOS ARE ALSO SEEN ON **RADAR**!
52
IN 1955, BETWEEN THE TOWNS OF KELLY AND **HOPKINSVILLE**, KENTUCKY, SOME FARMERS CLAIM TO HAVE SHOT AT ALIENS FROM A FLYING SAUCER!
I HIT THE CRITTER, BUT THE SHOT BOUNCED RIGHT OFF HIM!
THE SAME KIND OF CREATURE WAS SEEN IN FRANCE IN 1954 AND IN ARIZONA IN 1950.

MANY PEOPLE THINK UFO WITNESSES ARE NUTS.

UFOLOGISTS FIND MOSTLY ORDINARY PEOPLE WHO'VE SEEN EXTRAORDINARY THINGS!

 ONE NIGHT IN 1961, **BETTY AND BARNEY HILL** SAW A STRANGE LIGHT. WHEN BARNEY USED BINOCULARS, HE SAW WINDOWS IN THIS "LIGHT!" THE HILLS HURRIED HOME.

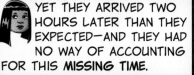 YET THEY ARRIVED TWO HOURS LATER THAN THEY EXPECTED—AND THEY HAD NO WAY OF ACCOUNTING FOR THIS **MISSING TIME.**

FOR NO REASON, BARNEY DEVELOPED A **RASH** ON HIS STOMACH, AND BETTY KEPT HAVING THE SAME STRANGE **NIGHTMARE!**

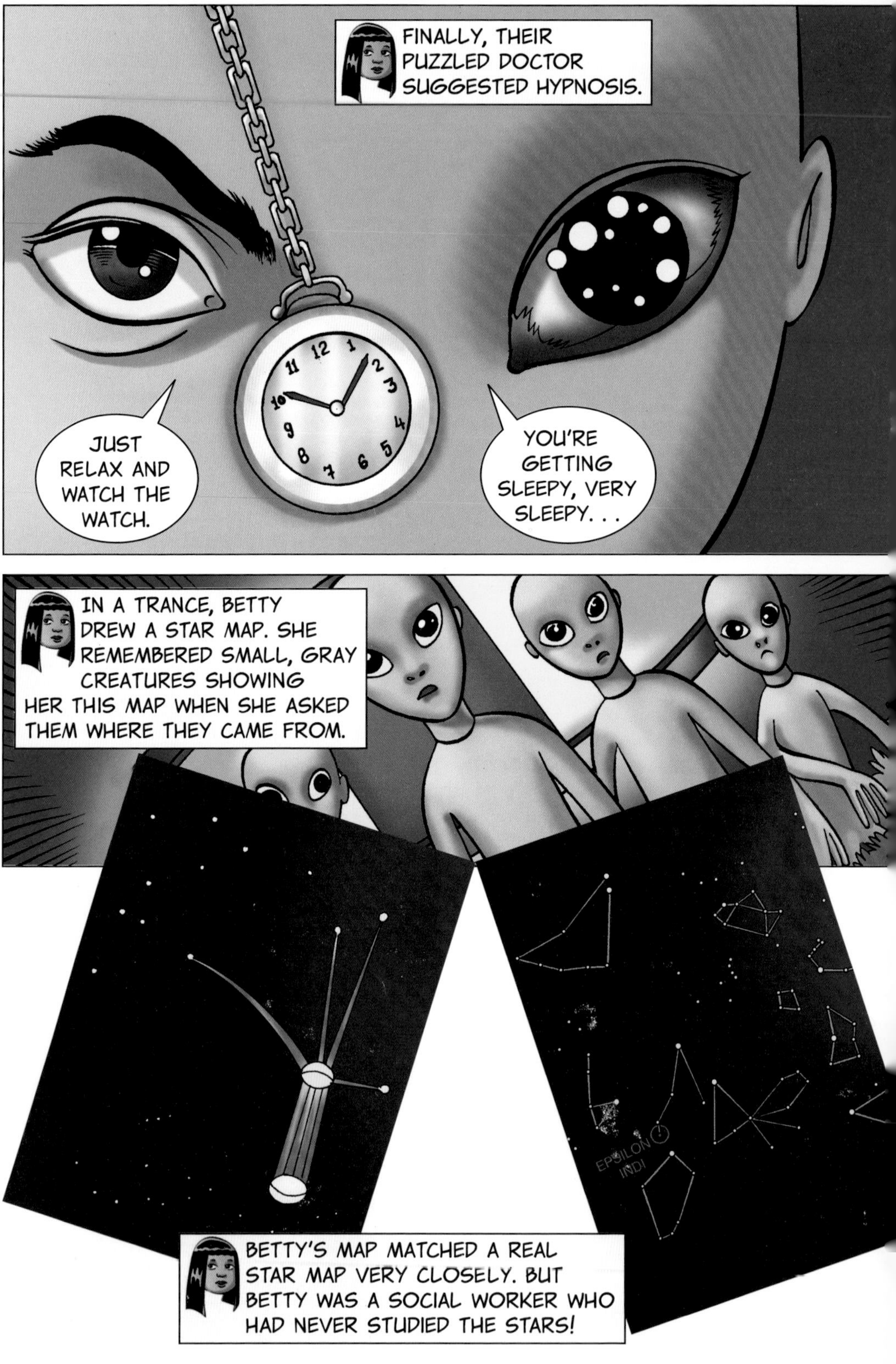
FINALLY, THEIR PUZZLED DOCTOR SUGGESTED HYPNOSIS.
JUST RELAX AND WATCH THE WATCH.
YOU'RE GETTING SLEEPY, VERY SLEEPY. . .
IN A TRANCE, BETTY DREW A STAR MAP. SHE REMEMBERED SMALL, GRAY CREATURES SHOWING HER THIS MAP WHEN SHE ASKED THEM WHERE THEY CAME FROM.
EPSILON INDI
BETTY'S MAP MATCHED A REAL STAR MAP VERY CLOSELY. BUT BETTY WAS A SOCIAL WORKER WHO HAD NEVER STUDIED THE STARS!

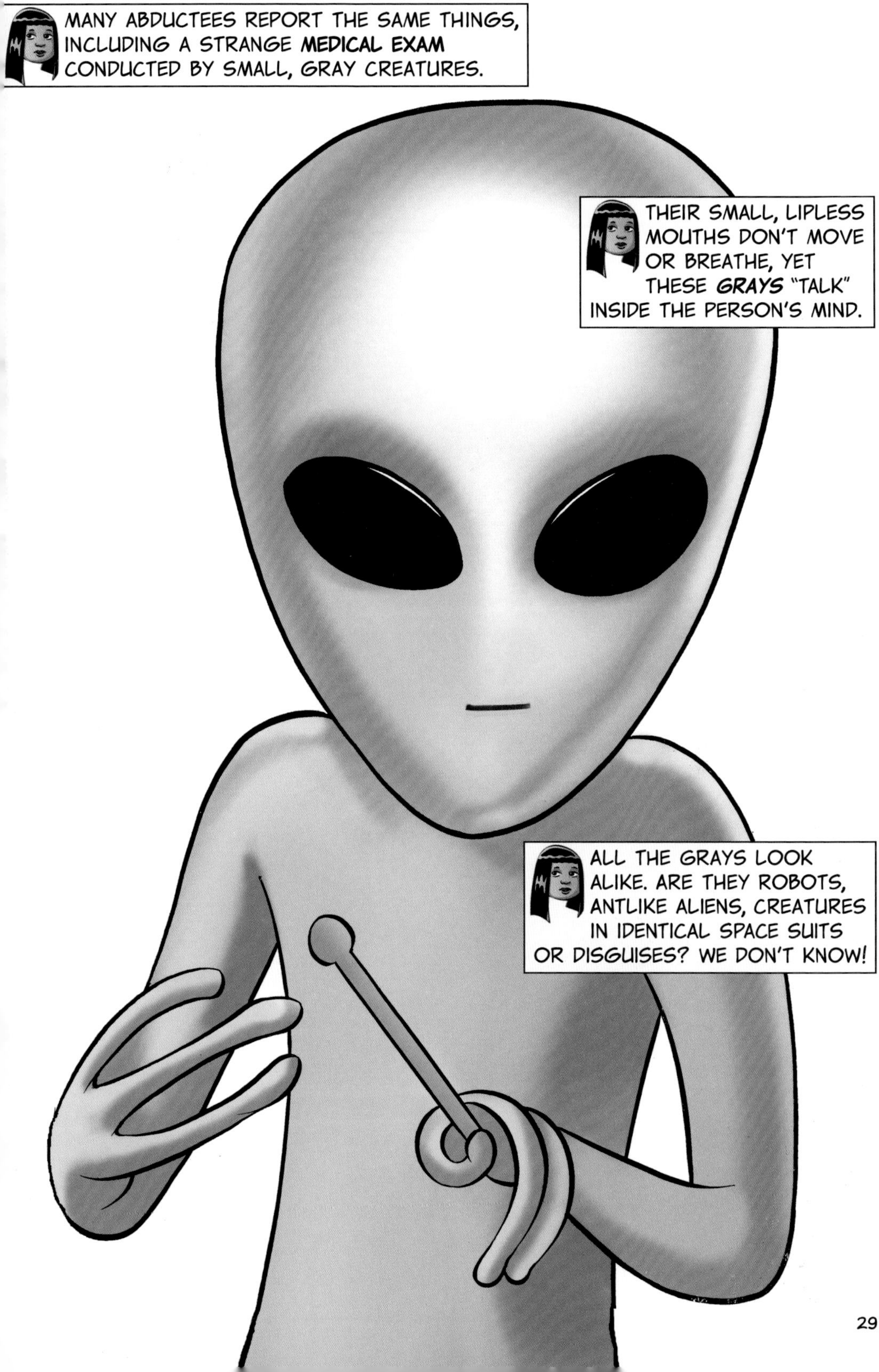
MANY ABDUCTEES REPORT THE SAME THINGS, INCLUDING A STRANGE **MEDICAL EXAM** CONDUCTED BY SMALL, GRAY CREATURES.
THEIR SMALL, LIPLESS MOUTHS DON'T MOVE OR BREATHE, YET THESE ***GRAYS*** "TALK" INSIDE THE PERSON'S MIND.
ALL THE GRAYS LOOK ALIKE. ARE THEY ROBOTS, ANTLIKE ALIENS, CREATURES IN IDENTICAL SPACE SUITS OR DISGUISES? WE DON'T KNOW!

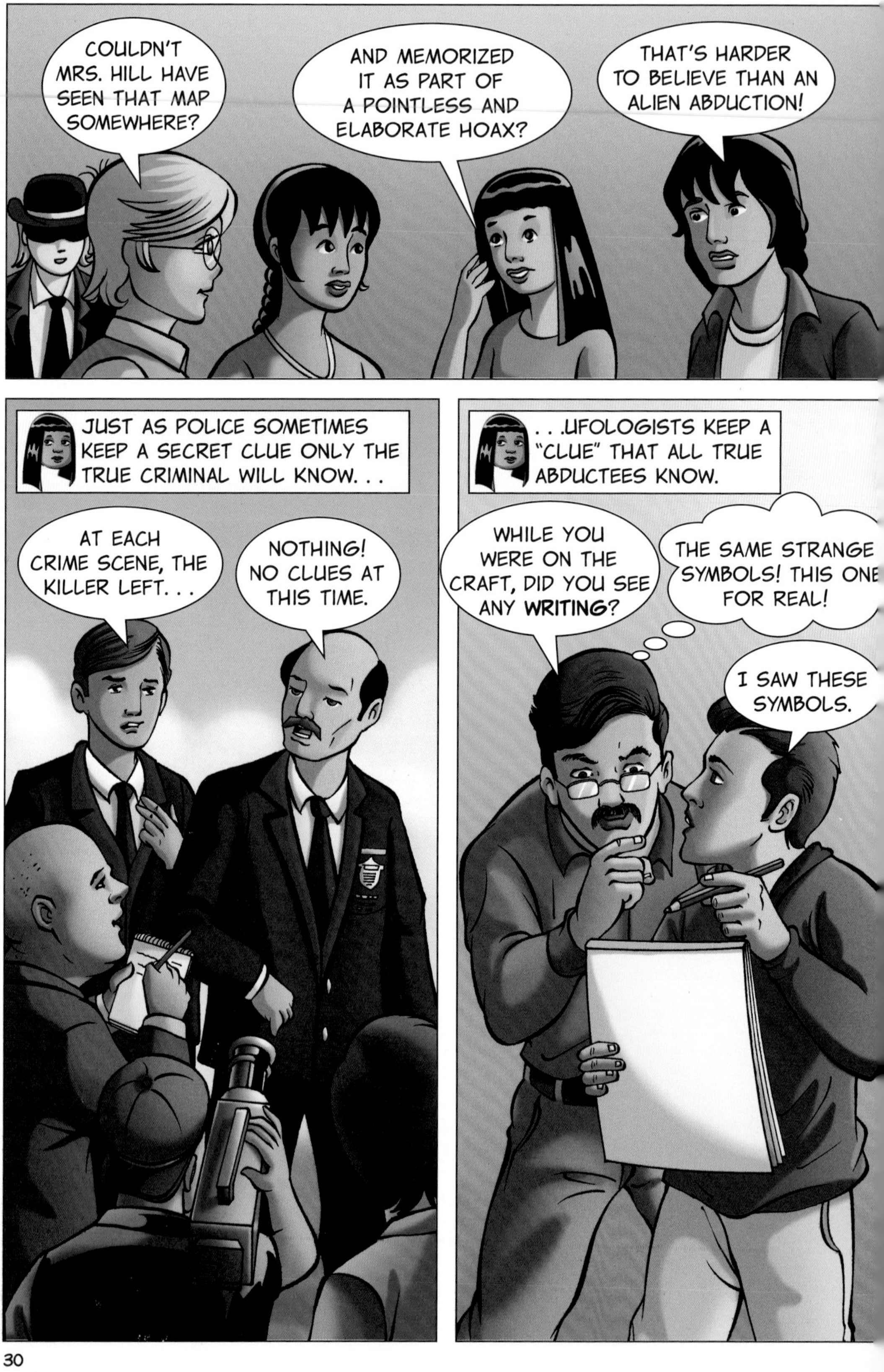
COULDN'T MRS. HILL HAVE SEEN THAT MAP SOMEWHERE?
AND MEMORIZED IT AS PART OF A POINTLESS AND ELABORATE HOAX?
THAT'S HARDER TO BELIEVE THAN AN ALIEN ABDUCTION!
JUST AS POLICE SOMETIMES KEEP A SECRET CLUE ONLY THE TRUE CRIMINAL WILL KNOW. . .
AT EACH CRIME SCENE, THE KILLER LEFT. . .
NOTHING! NO CLUES AT THIS TIME.
. . .UFOLOGISTS KEEP A "CLUE" THAT ALL TRUE ABDUCTEES KNOW.
WHILE YOU WERE ON THE CRAFT, DID YOU SEE ANY **WRITING**?
THE SAME STRANGE SYMBOLS! THIS ONE FOR REAL!
I SAW THESE SYMBOLS.

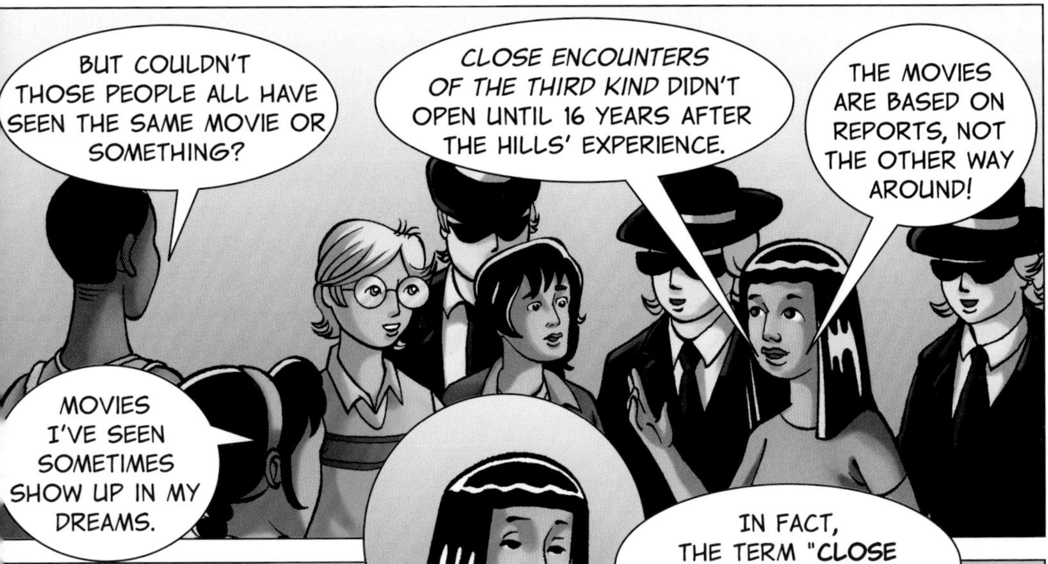
BUT COULDN'T THOSE PEOPLE ALL HAVE SEEN THE SAME MOVIE OR SOMETHING?
CLOSE ENCOUNTERS OF THE THIRD KIND DIDN'T OPEN UNTIL 16 YEARS AFTER THE HILLS' EXPERIENCE.
THE MOVIES ARE BASED ON REPORTS, NOT THE OTHER WAY AROUND!
MOVIES I'VE SEEN SOMETIMES SHOW UP IN MY DREAMS.
IN FACT, THE TERM "**CLOSE ENCOUNTER**" WASN'T EVEN INVENTED UNTIL 1972!

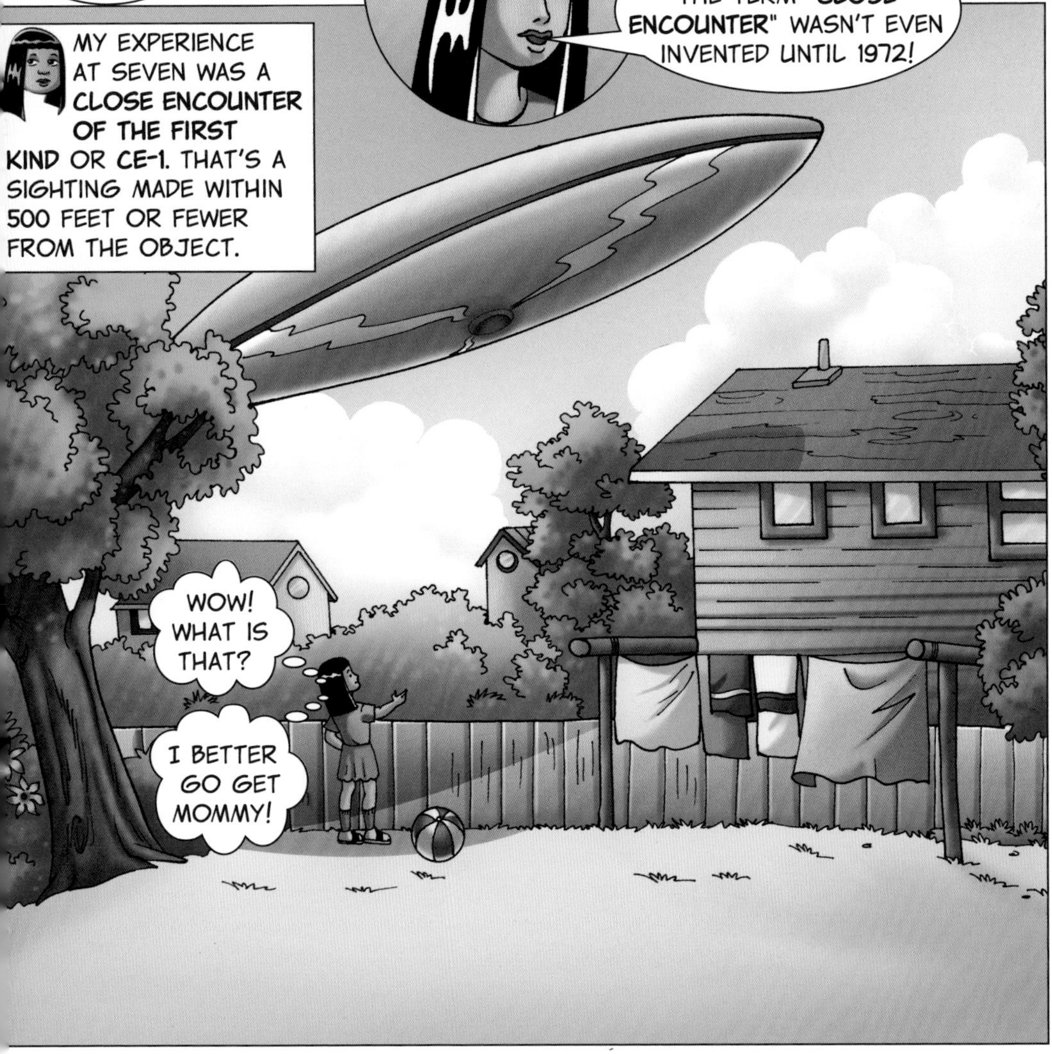
MY EXPERIENCE AT SEVEN WAS A **CLOSE ENCOUNTER OF THE FIRST KIND** OR **CE-1**. THAT'S A SIGHTING MADE WITHIN 500 FEET OR FEWER FROM THE OBJECT.
WOW! WHAT IS THAT?
I BETTER GO GET MOMMY!

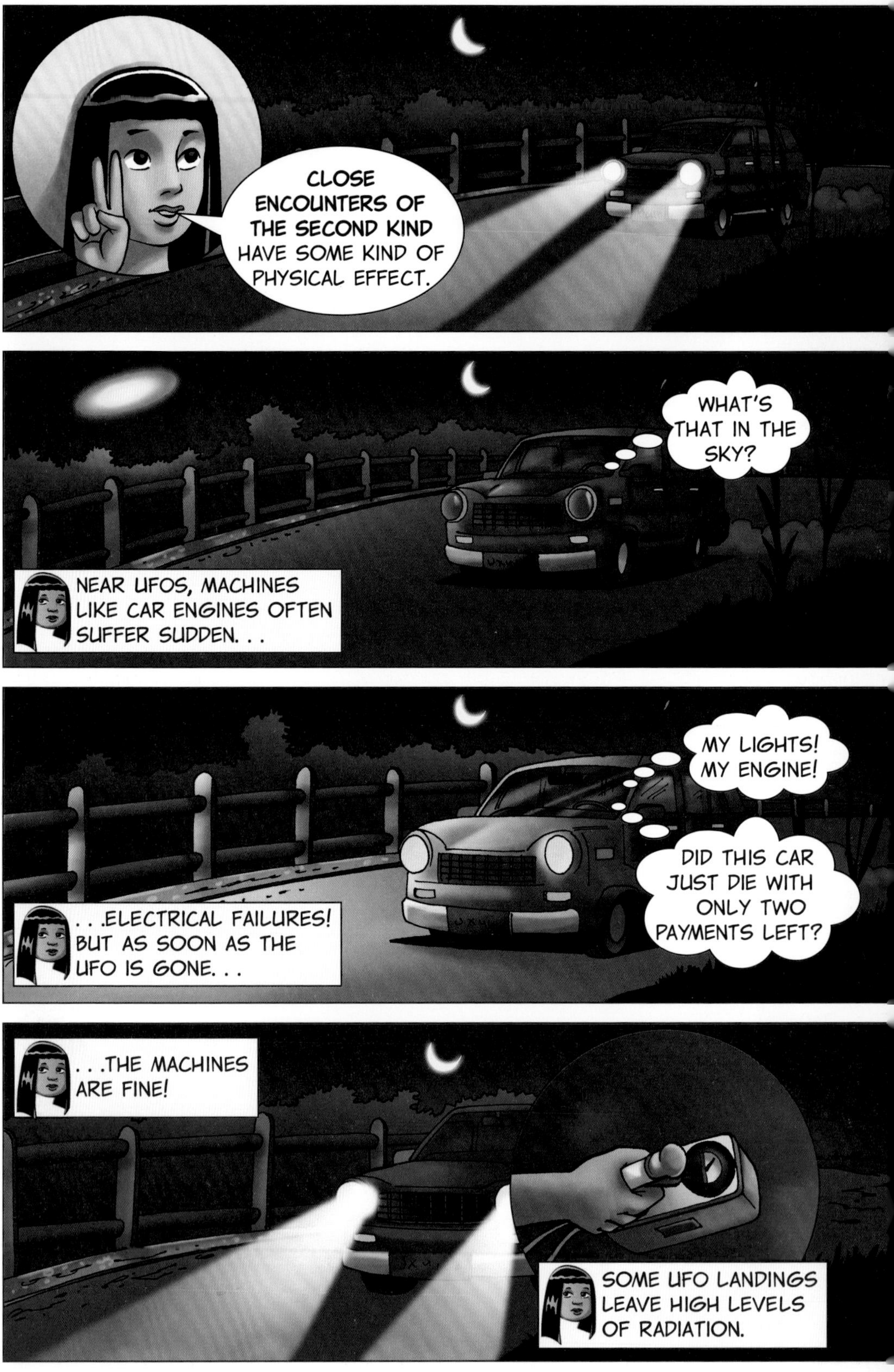
CLOSE ENCOUNTERS OF THE SECOND KIND HAVE SOME KIND OF PHYSICAL EFFECT.
WHAT'S THAT IN THE SKY?
NEAR UFOS, MACHINES LIKE CAR ENGINES OFTEN SUFFER SUDDEN. . .
MY LIGHTS! MY ENGINE!
DID THIS CAR JUST DIE WITH ONLY TWO PAYMENTS LEFT?
. . .ELECTRICAL FAILURES! BUT AS SOON AS THE UFO IS GONE. . .
. . .THE MACHINES ARE FINE!
SOME UFO LANDINGS LEAVE HIGH LEVELS OF RADIATION.

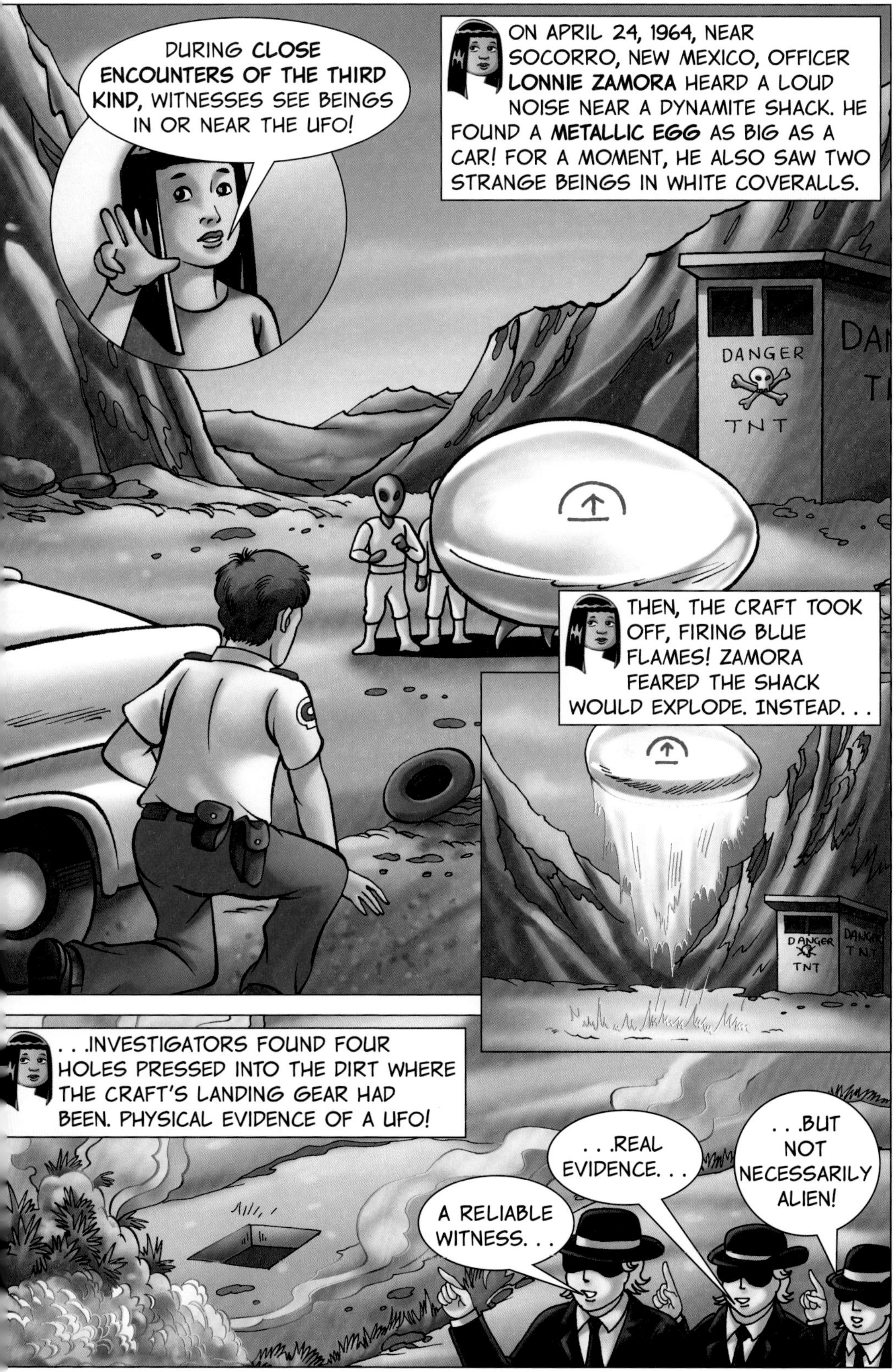
DURING CLOSE ENCOUNTERS OF THE THIRD KIND, WITNESSES SEE BEINGS IN OR NEAR THE UFO!
ON APRIL 24, 1964, NEAR SOCORRO, NEW MEXICO, OFFICER LONNIE ZAMORA HEARD A LOUD NOISE NEAR A DYNAMITE SHACK. HE FOUND A METALLIC EGG AS BIG AS A CAR! FOR A MOMENT, HE ALSO SAW TWO STRANGE BEINGS IN WHITE COVERALLS.
DANGER
TNT
THEN, THE CRAFT TOOK OFF, FIRING BLUE FLAMES! ZAMORA FEARED THE SHACK WOULD EXPLODE. INSTEAD. . .
DANGER
TNT
. . .INVESTIGATORS FOUND FOUR HOLES PRESSED INTO THE DIRT WHERE THE CRAFT'S LANDING GEAR HAD BEEN. PHYSICAL EVIDENCE OF A UFO!
A RELIABLE WITNESS. . .
. . .REAL EVIDENCE. . .
. . .BUT NOT NECESSARILY ALIEN!

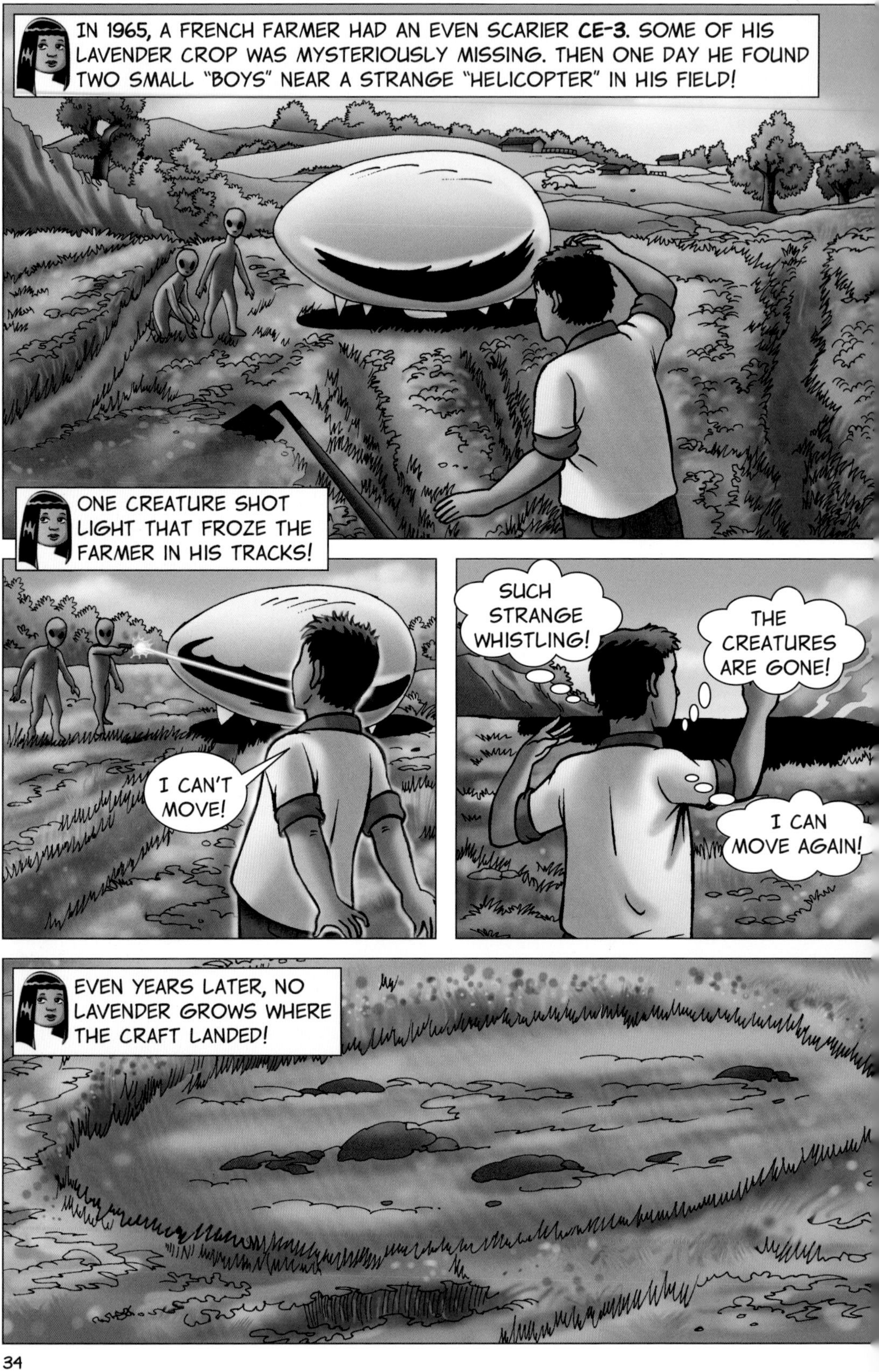
IN 1965, A FRENCH FARMER HAD AN EVEN SCARIER CE-3. SOME OF HIS LAVENDER CROP WAS MYSTERIOUSLY MISSING. THEN ONE DAY HE FOUND TWO SMALL "BOYS" NEAR A STRANGE "HELICOPTER" IN HIS FIELD!
ONE CREATURE SHOT LIGHT THAT FROZE THE FARMER IN HIS TRACKS!
I CAN'T MOVE!
SUCH STRANGE WHISTLING!
THE CREATURES ARE GONE!
I CAN MOVE AGAIN!
EVEN YEARS LATER, NO LAVENDER GROWS WHERE THE CRAFT LANDED!

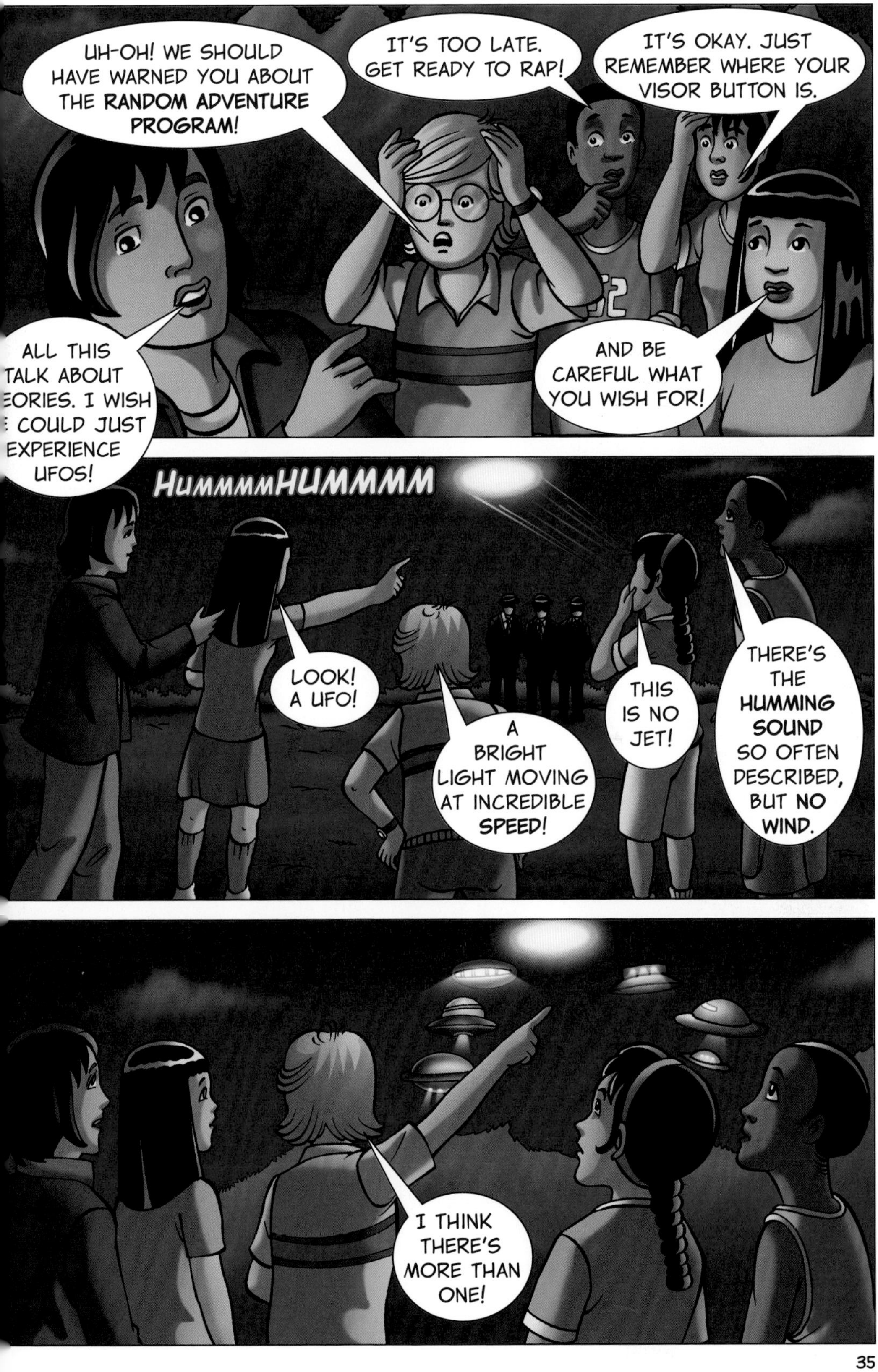
UH-OH! WE SHOULD HAVE WARNED YOU ABOUT THE **RANDOM ADVENTURE PROGRAM!**
IT'S TOO LATE. GET READY TO RAP!
IT'S OKAY. JUST REMEMBER WHERE YOUR VISOR BUTTON IS.
ALL THIS TALK ABOUT EORIES. I WISH COULD JUST EXPERIENCE UFOS!
AND BE CAREFUL WHAT YOU WISH FOR!
HummmmHUMMMM
LOOK! A UFO!
A BRIGHT LIGHT MOVING AT INCREDIBLE **SPEED!**
THIS IS NO JET!
THERE'S THE **HUMMING SOUND** SO OFTEN DESCRIBED, BUT **NO WIND.**
I THINK THERE'S MORE THAN ONE!

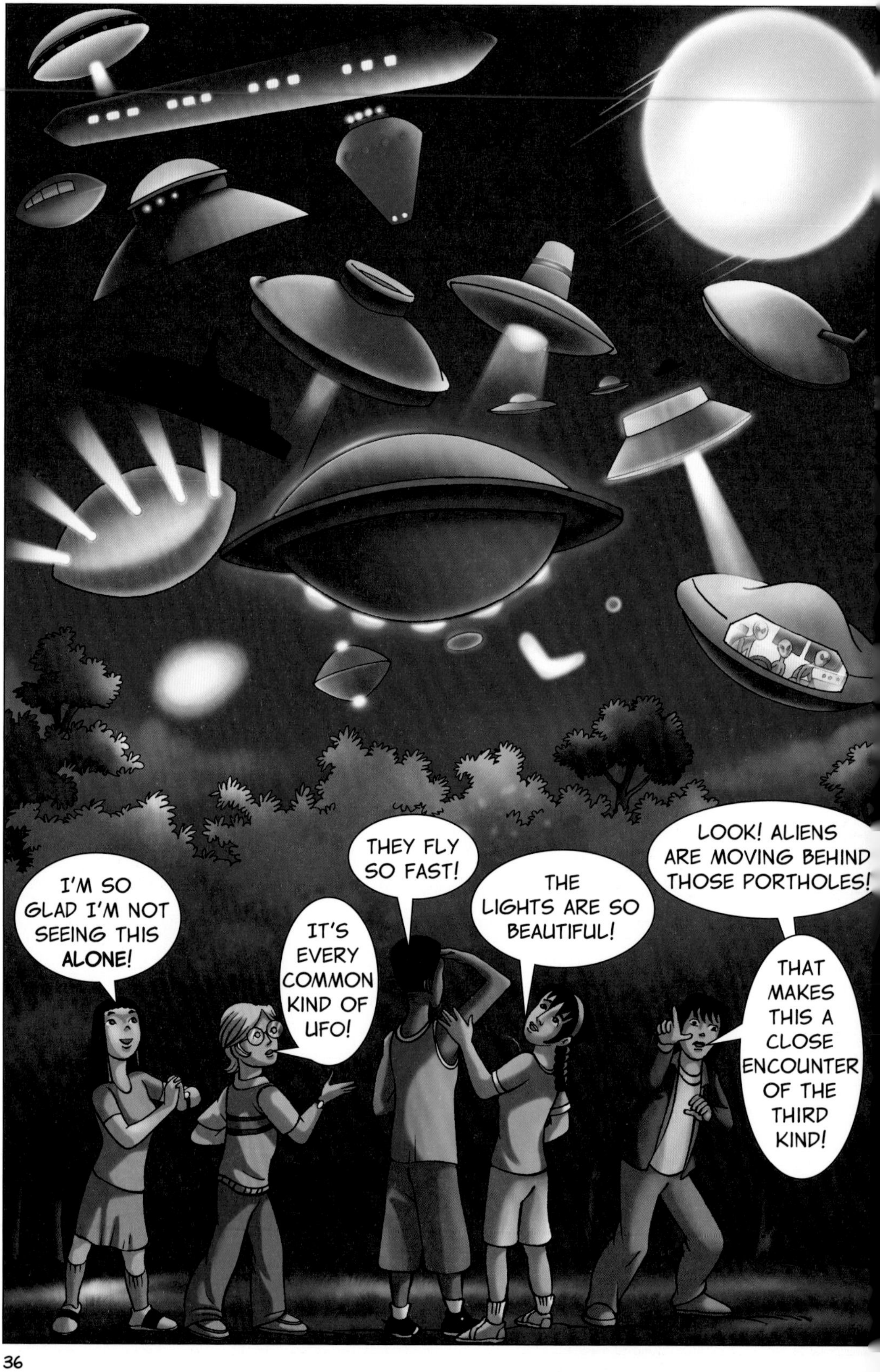
I'M SO GLAD I'M NOT SEEING THIS ALONE!
IT'S EVERY COMMON KIND OF UFO!
THEY FLY SO FAST!
THE LIGHTS ARE SO BEAUTIFUL!
LOOK! ALIENS ARE MOVING BEHIND THOSE PORTHOLES!
THAT MAKES THIS A CLOSE ENCOUNTER OF THE THIRD KIND!

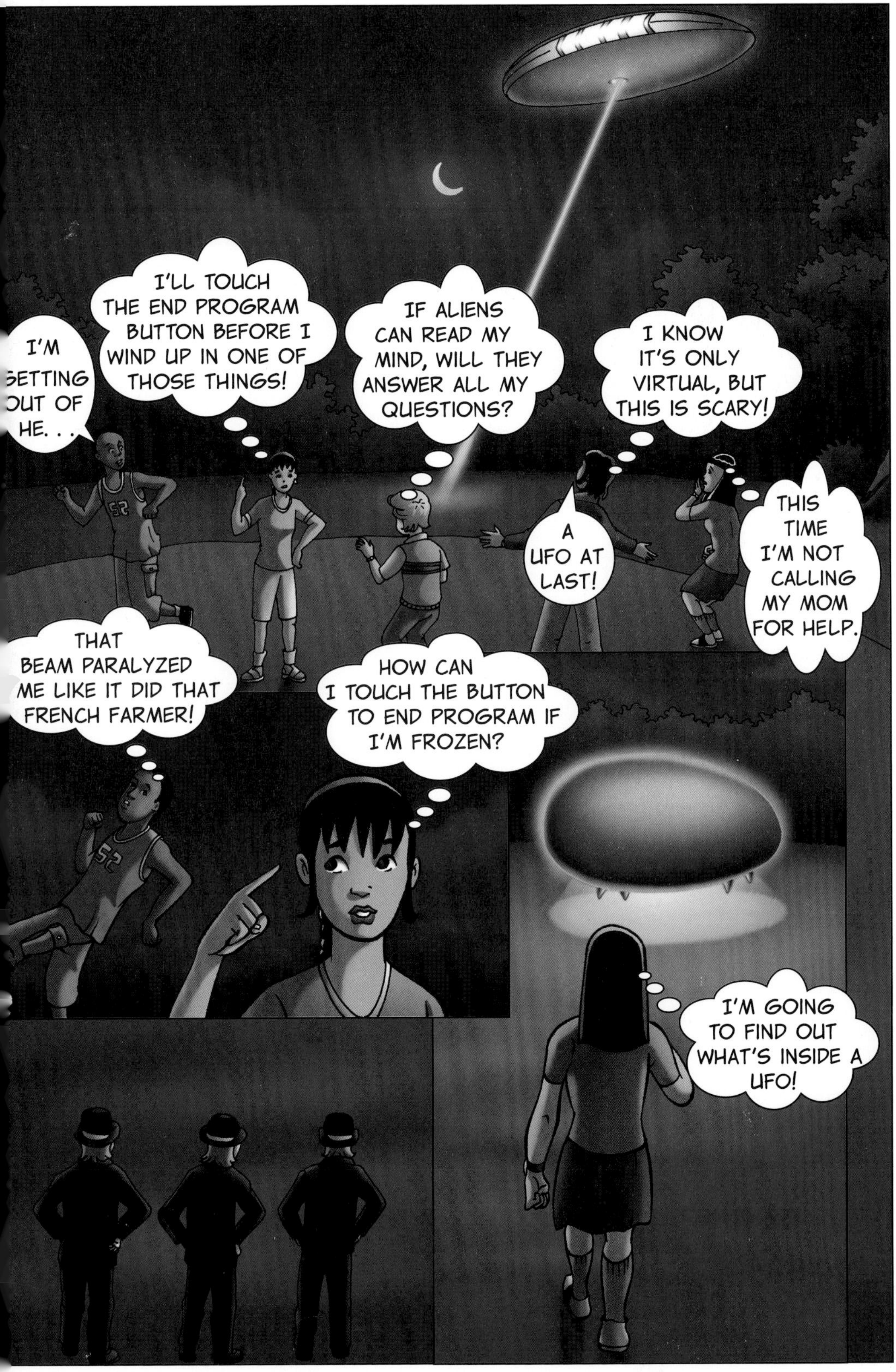

I'M GETTING OUT OF HE. . .
I'LL TOUCH THE END PROGRAM BUTTON BEFORE I WIND UP IN ONE OF THOSE THINGS!
IF ALIENS CAN READ MY MIND, WILL THEY ANSWER ALL MY QUESTIONS?
A UFO AT LAST!
I KNOW IT'S ONLY VIRTUAL, BUT THIS IS SCARY!
THIS TIME I'M NOT CALLING MY MOM FOR HELP.
THAT BEAM PARALYZED ME LIKE IT DID THAT FRENCH FARMER!
HOW CAN I TOUCH THE BUTTON TO END PROGRAM IF I'M FROZEN?
I'M GOING TO FIND OUT WHAT'S INSIDE A UFO!

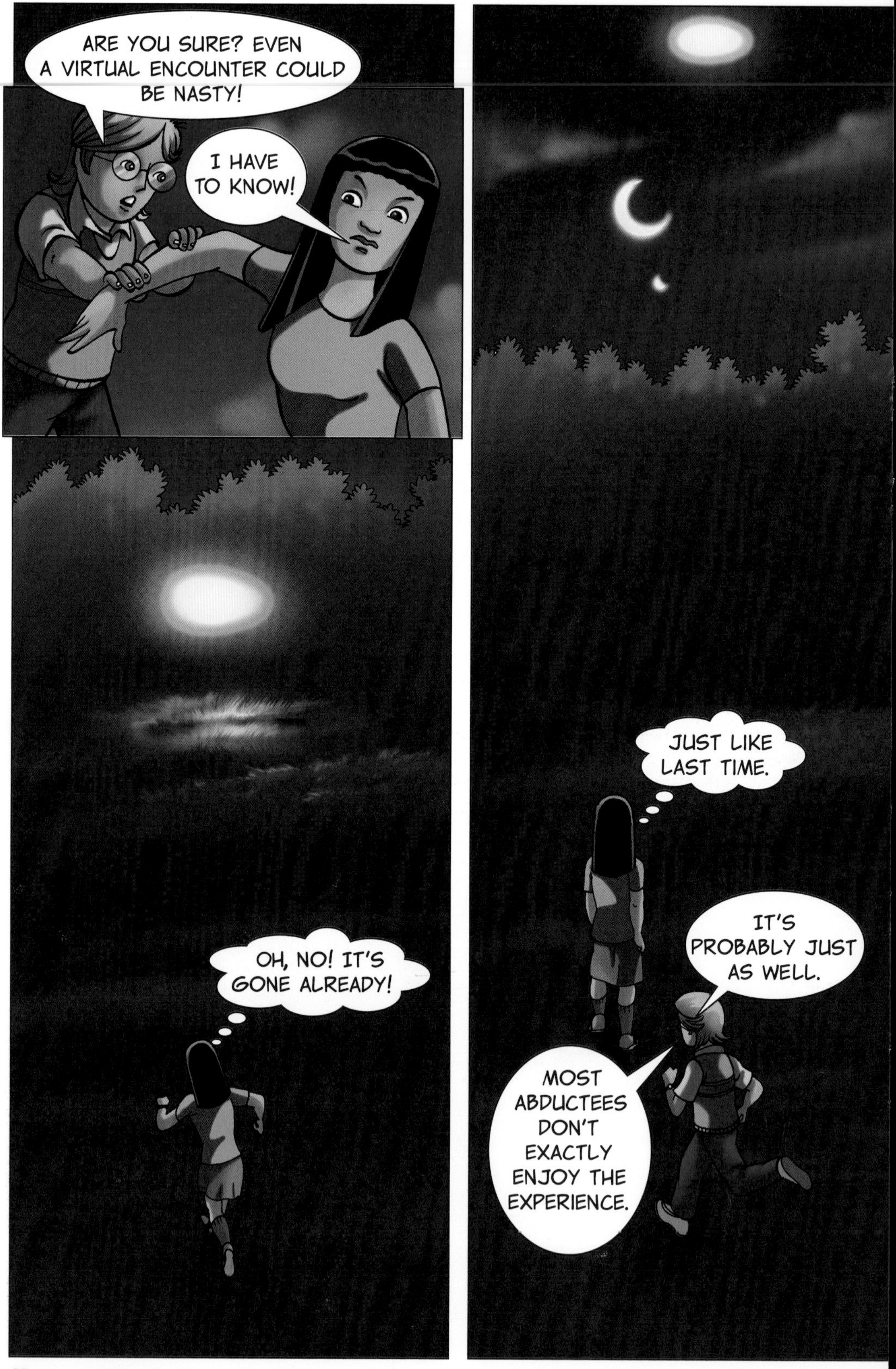
ARE YOU SURE? EVEN A VIRTUAL ENCOUNTER COULD BE NASTY!
I HAVE TO KNOW!
OH, NO! IT'S GONE ALREADY!
JUST LIKE LAST TIME.
IT'S PROBABLY JUST AS WELL.
MOST ABDUCTEES DON'T EXACTLY ENJOY THE EXPERIENCE.

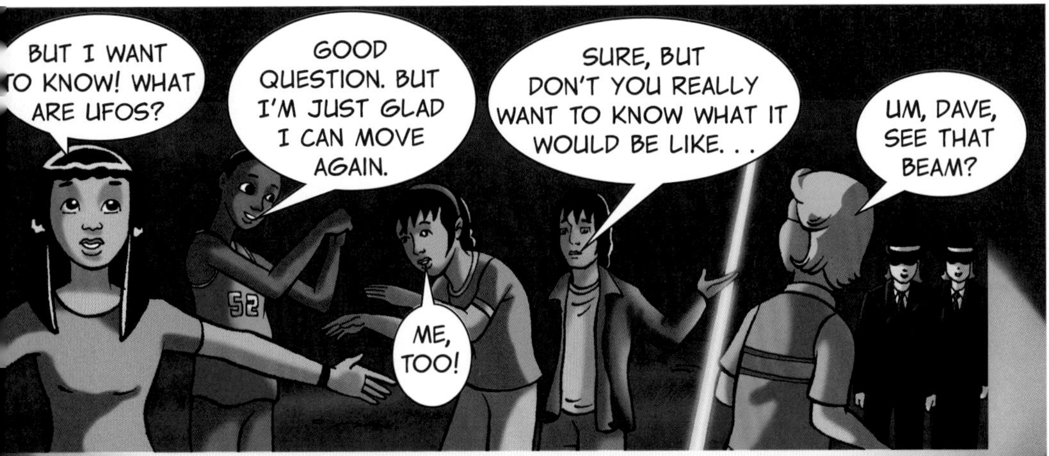
BUT I WANT TO KNOW! WHAT ARE UFOS?
GOOD QUESTION. BUT I'M JUST GLAD I CAN MOVE AGAIN.
ME, TOO!
SURE, BUT DON'T YOU REALLY WANT TO KNOW WHAT IT WOULD BE LIKE. . .
UM, DAVE, SEE THAT BEAM?

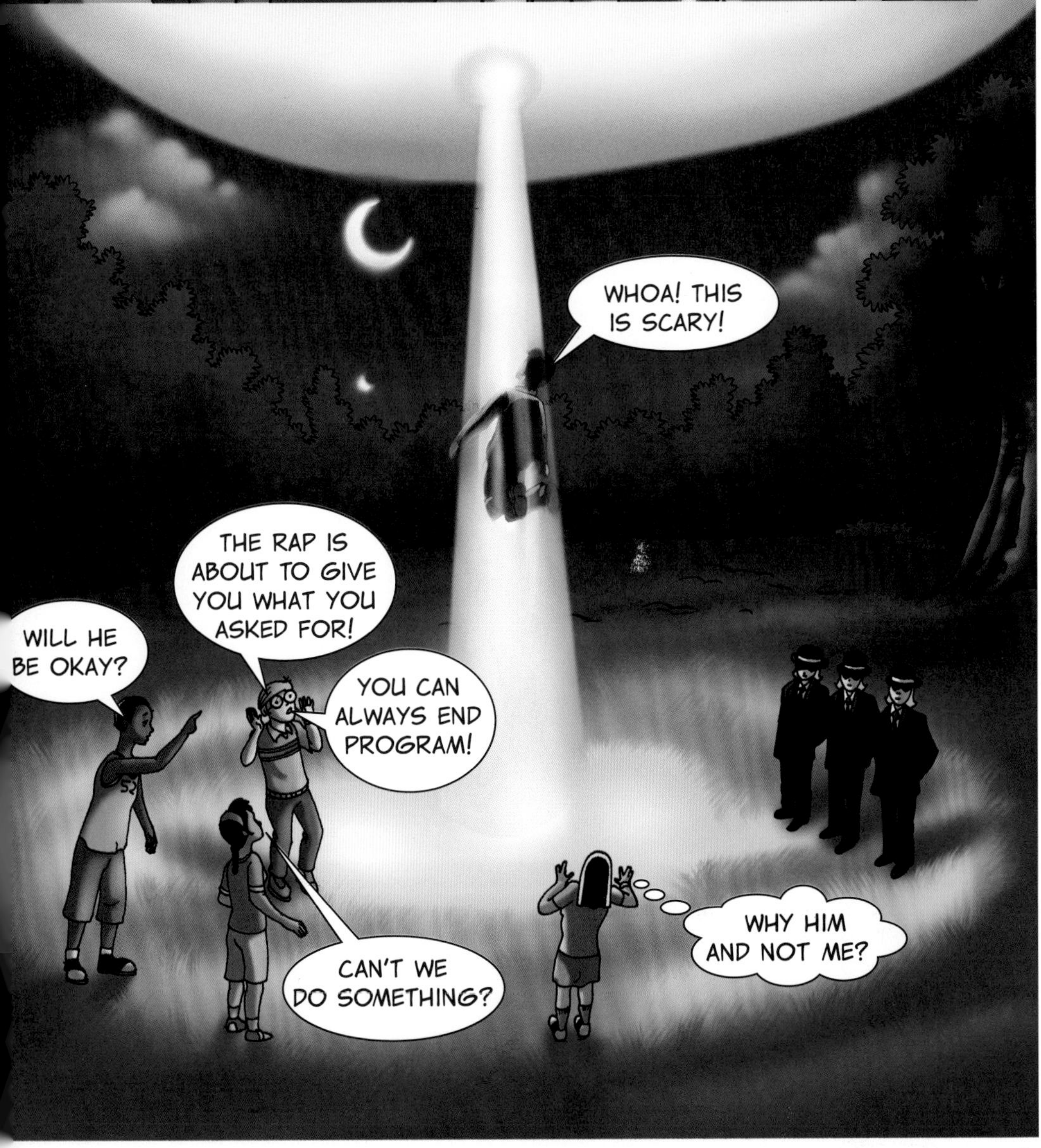
WHOA! THIS IS SCARY!
WILL HE BE OKAY?
THE RAP IS ABOUT TO GIVE YOU WHAT YOU ASKED FOR!
YOU CAN ALWAYS END PROGRAM!
CAN'T WE DO SOMETHING?
WHY HIM AND NOT ME?

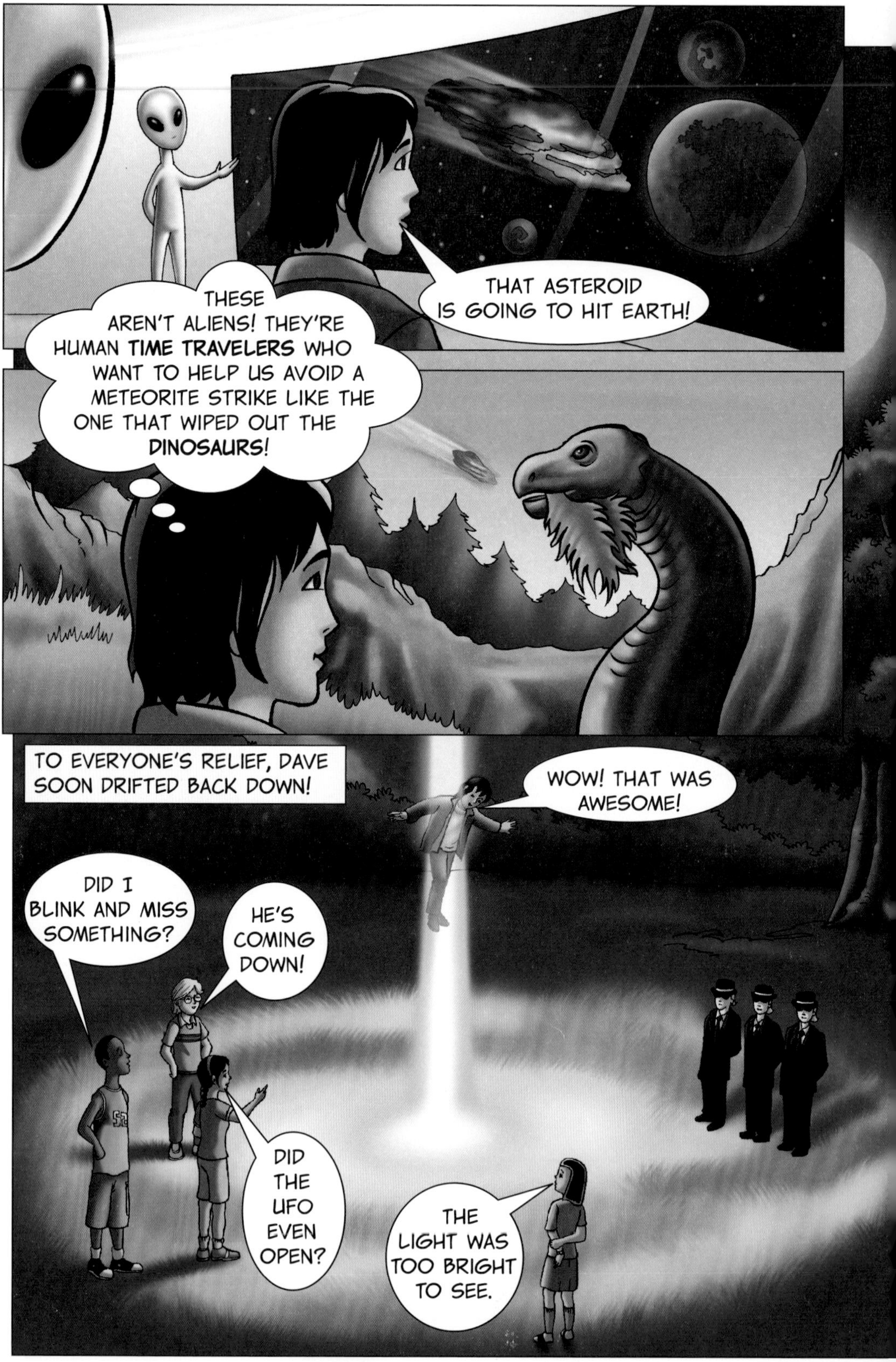
THAT ASTEROID IS GOING TO HIT EARTH!
THESE AREN'T ALIENS! THEY'RE HUMAN **TIME TRAVELERS** WHO WANT TO HELP US AVOID A METEORITE STRIKE LIKE THE ONE THAT WIPED OUT THE **DINOSAURS**!
TO EVERYONE'S RELIEF, DAVE SOON DRIFTED BACK DOWN!
WOW! THAT WAS AWESOME!
DID I BLINK AND MISS SOMETHING?
HE'S COMING DOWN!
DID THE UFO EVEN OPEN?
THE LIGHT WAS TOO BRIGHT TO SEE.

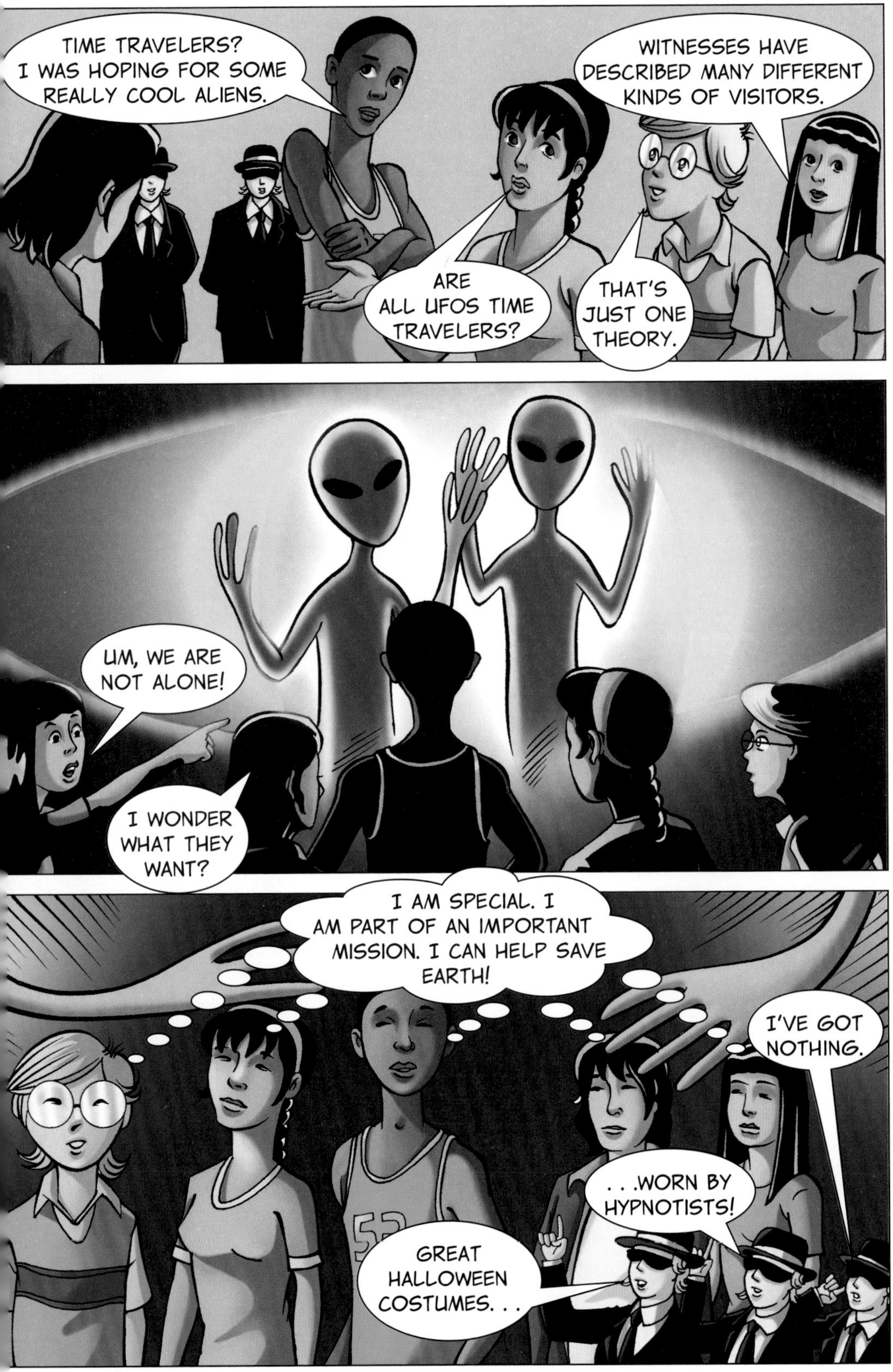
TIME TRAVELERS? I WAS HOPING FOR SOME REALLY COOL ALIENS.
WITNESSES HAVE DESCRIBED MANY DIFFERENT KINDS OF VISITORS.
ARE ALL UFOS TIME TRAVELERS?
THAT'S JUST ONE THEORY.
UM, WE ARE NOT ALONE!
I WONDER WHAT THEY WANT?
I AM SPECIAL. I AM PART OF AN IMPORTANT MISSION. I CAN HELP SAVE EARTH!
I'VE GOT NOTHING.
. . .WORN BY HYPNOTISTS!
GREAT HALLOWEEN COSTUMES. . .

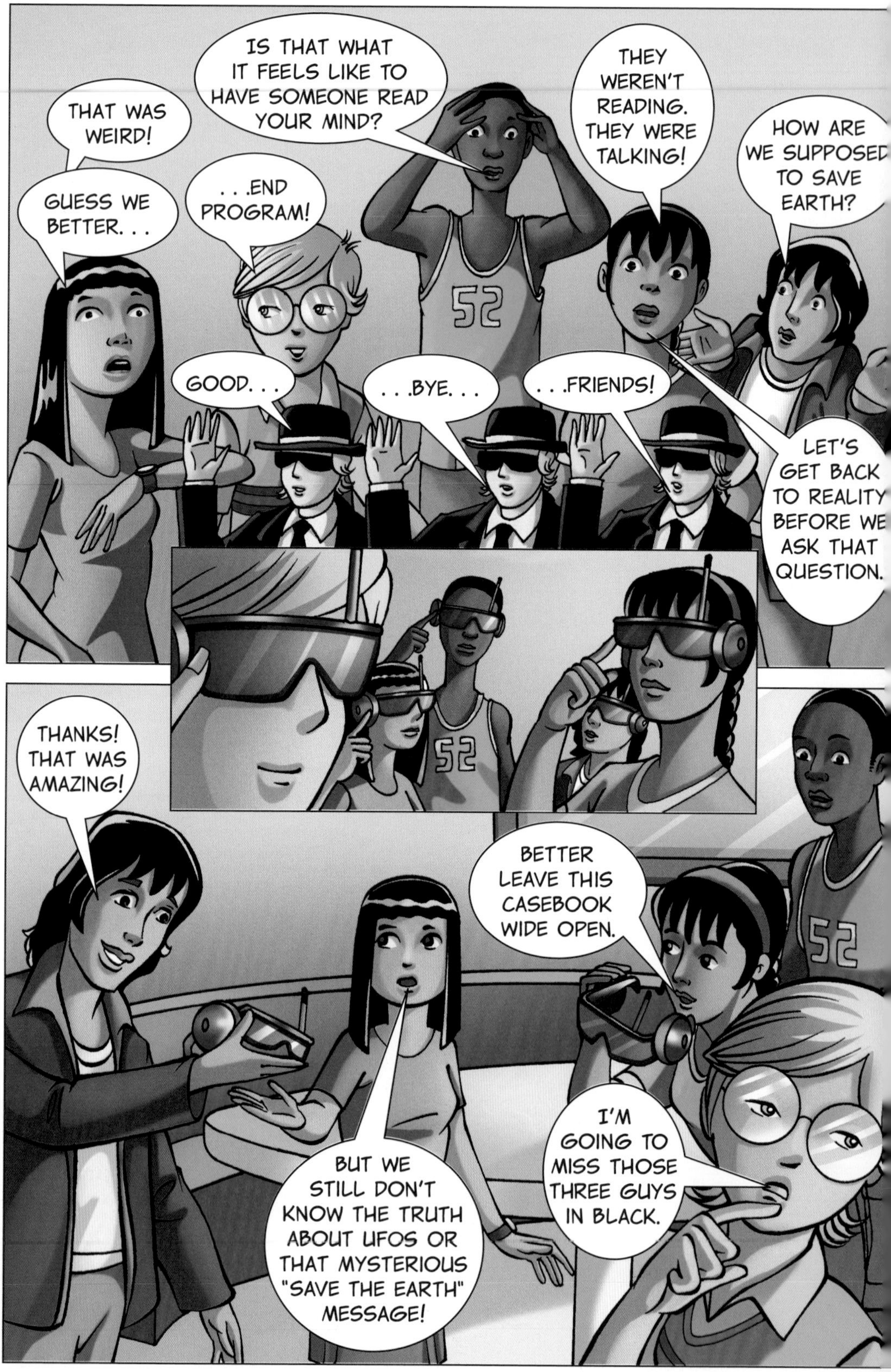
THAT WAS WEIRD!
GUESS WE BETTER. . .
. . .END PROGRAM!
IS THAT WHAT IT FEELS LIKE TO HAVE SOMEONE READ YOUR MIND?
THEY WEREN'T READING. THEY WERE TALKING!
HOW ARE WE SUPPOSED TO SAVE EARTH?
GOOD. . .
. . .BYE. . .
. . .FRIENDS!
LET'S GET BACK TO REALITY BEFORE WE ASK THAT QUESTION.
THANKS! THAT WAS AMAZING!
BETTER LEAVE THIS CASEBOOK WIDE OPEN.
BUT WE STILL DON'T KNOW THE TRUTH ABOUT UFOS OR THAT MYSTERIOUS "SAVE THE EARTH" MESSAGE!
I'M GOING TO MISS THOSE THREE GUYS IN BLACK.

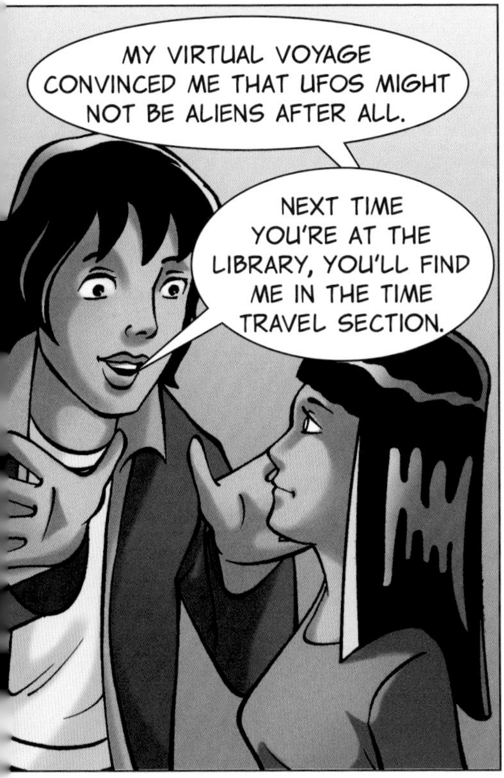
MY VIRTUAL VOYAGE CONVINCED ME THAT UFOS MIGHT NOT BE ALIENS AFTER ALL.
NEXT TIME YOU'RE AT THE LIBRARY, YOU'LL FIND ME IN THE TIME TRAVEL SECTION.

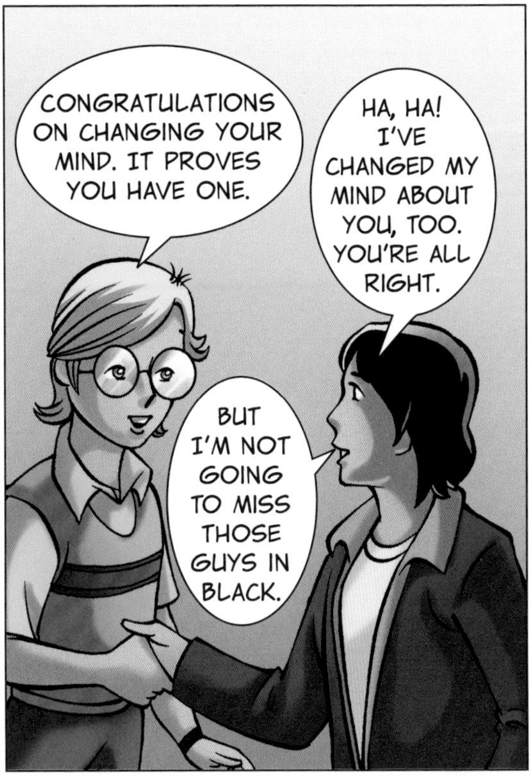
CONGRATULATIONS ON CHANGING YOUR MIND. IT PROVES YOU HAVE ONE.
HA, HA! I'VE CHANGED MY MIND ABOUT YOU, TOO. YOU'RE ALL RIGHT.
BUT I'M NOT GOING TO MISS THOSE GUYS IN BLACK.

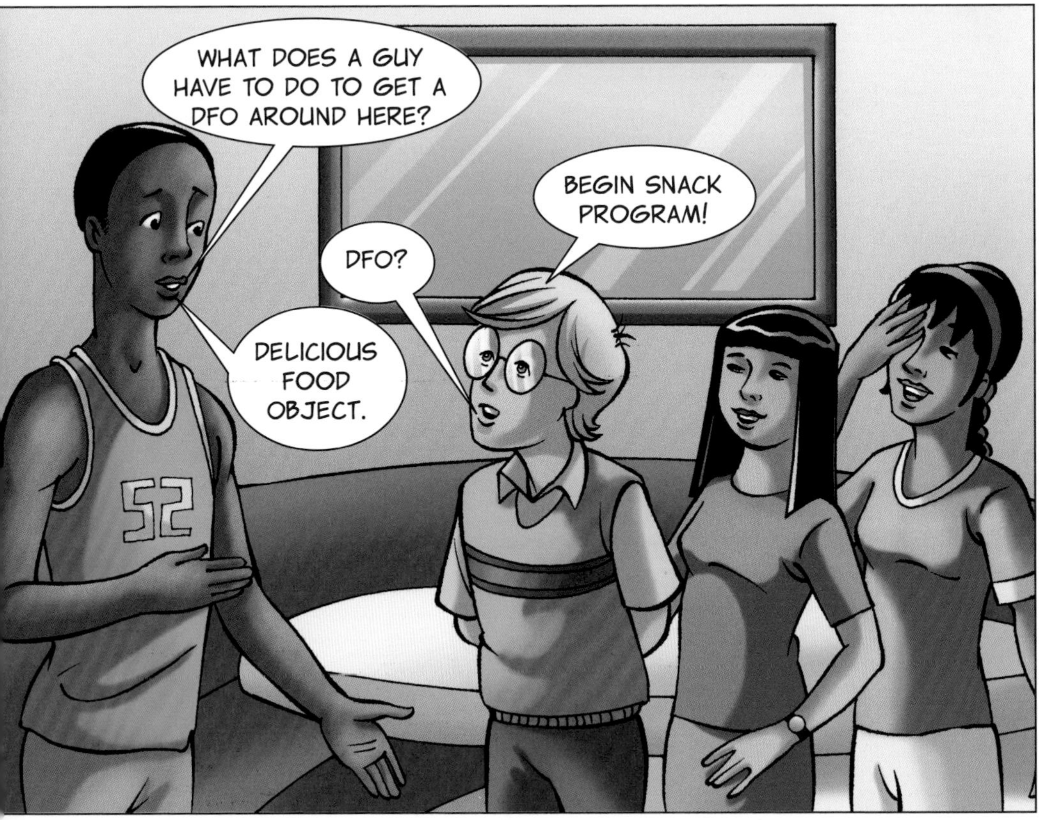
WHAT DOES A GUY HAVE TO DO TO GET A DFO AROUND HERE?
DFO?
DELICIOUS FOOD OBJECT.
BEGIN SNACK PROGRAM!

FACT FILE

Identified Flying Objects (IFOs): Many objects seen flying through the sky look like alien aircraft but aren't! Investigations have identified an amazing variety of other explanations. IFOs could fill a casebook themselves!

Parallel worlds: "Parallel" comes from the Greek *para* meaning "side-by-side" plus *allelios* meaning "one another." Meaning "extending in the same direction and at a constant distance apart so as never to meet, as in lines or planes; similar or corresponding to another; counterpart."

One theory about UFOs is that they are portals for travelers from parallel dimensions. Could each person living on Earth right now have a counterpart living a slightly different life in a parallel world? No evidence yet exists to support this theory.

FACT FILE

Technology: From the Greek *techne* meaning "a craft, mixing art, science and skill;" and the Greek *logos* meaning a "word." A practical application of science. As Edward Icarus Stein likes to say, "Technology is science in action!"

Humans and some other animals on Earth use tools. The theory that aliens helped people develop technology has not yet been proven.

Dirigible: A small, non-rigid or semi-rigid airship; sometimes called by the nickname *blimp*, from the Latin *dirigere* meaning "to make straight" or "to direct." A balloonlike airship that can be steered. They are often long, shaped like a cigar, motor driven, and with a cabin underneath. A blimp is a nonrigid airship. Some UFOs that turn out to be IFOs are blimps.

Antigravity: The prefix "anti" is from the Greek word meaning "against." "Gravity" is from the Latin *gravis* meaning "heavy." In physics, gravity is the force that tends to draw all bodies in Earth's sphere toward the center of Earth. Gravity also pulls planets and stars toward each other.

Some people believe UFOs can travel faster than light because they somehow overcome gravity and friction, and, unlike jet engines, they do not depend on moving air. This would explain why witnesses often report that UFOs are much quieter than jets.

FACT FILE

Meteor: From the Greek *meteora* meaning "things in the air." Any of the many small, solid bodies traveling through space, visible as a bright streak of light as it enters Earth's atmosphere. Meteors look bright because of the white-hot friction generated by their speedy entry into the atmosphere. "Shooting star" is a nickname for a meteor. Most meteors burn up before they hit the ground, but any that reach Earth are called **meteorites**. Some UFOs turn out to be IFOs when they are proven to be meteors.

WHOA! THIS IS SCARY!

Abductee: "Abduct" comes from the Latin *ab* meaning "away" and *ducere* meaning "to lead." "To abduct" means "to kidnap." "Ee" is a noun-forming suffix that means "the receiver of an action or benefit." Abductees are people who claim to have been carried off by aliens against their will.

One abductee went to a psychologist for help. He was disappointed when the doctor told him he *wasn't* crazy. Why was he disappointed? Mental illness can be cured. But what can you do about being abducted by aliens?

Find Out for Yourself

UFOs touch on many fascinating subjects. You might feel inspired to create your own casebook by looking up topics like these:

- The history of human flight

- Missing time and UFOs

- Telepathy and UFOs

- Radiation sickness and cures and UFOs

- The use of hypnosis to recover lost memories and UFOs

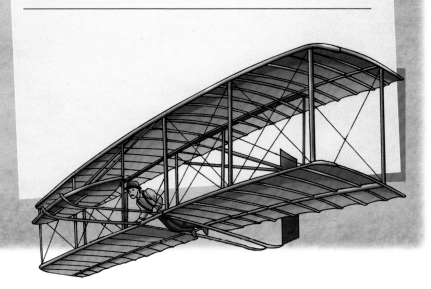

Web Sites

To ensure the currency and safety of recommended Internet links, Windmill maintains and updates an online list of sites related to the subject of this book. To access this list of Web sites, please go to **www.windmillbks.com/weblinks** and select this book's title.

About the Author/Artist

Justine and Ron Fontes met at a publishing house in New York City, where he worked for the comic book department and she was an editorial assistant in children's books. Together, they have written over 500 children's books, in every format from board books to historical novels. They live in Maine, where they continue their work in writing and comics and publish a newsletter, *critter news*.

For more great fiction and nonfiction, go to www.windmillbooks.com